STEPHEN KING

MORALITY

SCRIBNER

New York   London   Toronto   Sydney

SCRIBNER
A Division of Simon & Schuster, Inc.
1230 Avenue of the Americas
New York, NY 10020

First Scribner hardcover edition May 2010

SCRIBNER and design are registered trademarks of The Gale Group,
Inc., used under license by Simon & Schuster, Inc., the publisher of this work.

For information about special discounts for bulk purchases,
please contact Simon & Schuster Special Sales at 1-866-506-1949
or business@simonandschuster.com.

The Simon & Schuster Speakers Bureau can bring authors to your live event.
For more information or to book an event contact the Simon & Schuster
Speakers Bureau at 1-866-248-3049 or visit our website at
www.simonspeakers.com.

Manufactured in the United States of America

1   3   5   7   9   10   8   6   4   2

ISBN 978-1-4516-0821-2

Blockade Billy was first published in a limited hardcover edition
by Cemetery Dance Publications. http://www.cemeterydance.com.

"Morality" was first published in *Esquire*.

This is for every guy (and gal)
who ever put on the gear.

Contents

William Blakely?

Oh my God, you mean Blockade Billy. Nobody's asked me about him in years. Of course, no one asks me much of anything in here, except if I'd like to sign up for Polka Night at the K of P Hall downtown or something called Virtual Bowling. That's right here in the Common Room. My advice to you, Mr. King— you didn't ask for it, but I'll give it to you—is don't get old, and if you do, don't let your relatives put you in a zombie hotel like this one.

It's a funny thing, getting old. When you're young, people always want to listen to your stories, especially if you were in pro baseball. But when you're young, you don't have time to tell them. Now I've got all the time in the world, and it seems like nobody cares about those old days. But I still like to think about them. So sure, I'll tell you about Billy Blakely. Awful story, of course, but those are the ones that last the longest.

Baseball was different in those days. You have to remember that Blockade Billy played for the Titans only ten years after Jackie Robinson broke the color barrier, and the Titans are long gone. I don't suppose New Jersey will ever have another Major League team, not with two powerhouse franchises just across the river in New York. But it was a big deal then—*we* were a big deal—and we played our games in a different world.

The rules were the same. Those don't change. And the little rituals were pretty similar, too. Oh, nobody would have been allowed to wear their cap cocked to the side, or curve the brim, and your hair had to be neat and short (the way these chuckleheads wear it now, my God), but some players still crossed themselves before they stepped into the box, or drew in the dirt with the heads of their bats before taking up the stance, or jumped over the baseline when they were running out to take their positions. Nobody wanted to step on the baseline, it was considered the worst luck to do that.

The game was *local,* okay? TV had started to come in, but only on the weekends. We had a good market, because the games were on WNJ, and everyone in New York could watch. Some of those broadcasts were pretty comical. Compared to the way they do today's games, it was all amateur night in Dixie. Radio was better, more professional, but of course that was local, too. No satellite broadcasts, because there were no satellites! The Russians sent the first one up during the Yanks-Braves World Series that year. As I remember, it happened on an off-day, but I could be wrong about that. What I remember is that the Titans were out of it early that year. We contended for a while, partly thanks to Blockade Billy, but you know how *that* turned out. It's why you came, right?

But here's what I'm getting at: Because the game was smaller on the national stage, the players weren't such a big deal. I'm not saying there weren't stars—guys like Aaron, Burdette, Williams, Kaline, and of course The Mick—but most weren't as well-known coast to coast as players like Alex Rodriguez and Barry Bonds (a couple of bushers, if you ask me). And most of the other guys? I can tell you in two words: working stiffs. The average salary back then was fifteen grand, less than a first-year high school teacher makes today.

Working stiffs, get it? Just like George Will said in that book of his. Only he talked about that like it was a good thing. I'm not so sure it was, if you were a thirty-year-old shortstop with a wife and three kids and maybe another seven years to go before retirement. Ten, if you were lucky and didn't get hurt. Carl Furillo ended up installing elevators in the World Trade Center and moonlighting as a night watchman, did you know that? You did? Do you think that guy Will knew it, or just forgot to mention it?

The deal was this: If you had the skills and could do the job even with a hangover, you got to play. If you couldn't, you got tossed on the scrapheap. It was that simple. And as brutal. Which brings me to our catching situation that spring.

We were in good shape during camp, which for the Titans was in Sarasota. Our starting catcher was Johnny Goodkind. Maybe you don't remember him. If you do, it's probably because of the way he ended up. He had four good years, batted over .300, put the gear on almost every game. Knew how to handle the pitchers, didn't take any guff. The kids didn't dare shake him off. He hit damn near .350 that spring, with maybe a dozen ding-dongs, one as deep and far as any I ever saw at Ed Smith Stadium, where the ball didn't carry well. Put out the windshield in some reporter's Chevrolet—ha!

But he was also a big drinker, and two days before the team was supposed to head north and open at home, he ran over a woman on Pineapple Street and killed her just as dead as a dormouse. Or doornail. Whatever the saying is. Then the damn fool tried to run. But there was a County Sheriff's cruiser parked on the corner of Orange, and the deputies inside saw the whole thing. Wasn't much doubt about Johnny's state, either. When they pulled him out of his car, he smelled like a brewery and could hardly stand. One of the deputies bent down to put the cuffs on him, and Johnny threw up on the back of the guy's head. Johnny Goodkind's career in baseball was over before the puke dried. Even the Babe couldn't have stayed in the game after running over a housewife out doing her morning shop-around.

Stephen
King

His backup was a guy named Frank Faraday. Not bad behind the plate, but a banjo hitter at best. Went about one-fifty. No bulk, which put him at risk. The game was played hard in those days, Mr. King, with plenty of fuck-you.

But Faraday was what we had. I remember DiPunno saying he wouldn't last long, but not even Jersey Joe had an idea how short a time it was going to be.

Faraday was behind the plate when we played our last exhibition game that year. Against the Reds, it was. There was a squeeze play put on. Don Hoak at the plate. Some big hulk—I think it was Ted Kluszewski—on third. Hoak punches the ball right at Jerry Rugg, who was pitching for us that day. Big Klew breaks for the plate, all two hundred and seventy Polack pounds of him. And there's Faraday, just about as skinny as a Flav-R Straw, standing with one foot on the old dishola. You knew it was going to end bad. Rugg throws to Faraday. Faraday turns to put the tag on. I couldn't look.

Faraday hung on to the ball and got the out, I'll give him that, only it was a spring training out, as important in the great scheme of things as a low fart in a high wind. And that was the end of *his* baseball career. One broken arm, one broken leg, a concussion—that was the score. I don't know what became of him. Wound up washing windshields for tips at an Esso station in Tucumcari, for all I know. He wouldn't be the only one.

But here's the point: We lost both our catchers in the space of forty-eight hours and had to go north with nobody to put behind the plate except for Ganzie Burgess, who converted from catcher to pitcher in the early fifties. He was thirty-nine years old that season and only good for middle relief, but he was a knuckleballer, and as crafty as Satan, so no way was Joe DiPunno going to risk those old bones behind the plate. He said he'd put *me* back there first. I knew he was joking—I was just an old third-base coach with so many groin-pulls my balls were practically banging on my knees—but the idea still made me shiver.

What Joe did was call the front office in Newark and say, "I need a guy who can catch Hank Masters's fastball and Danny Doo's curve without falling on

his keister. I don't care if he plays for Testicle Tire in Tremont, just make sure he's got a mitt and have him at The Swamp in time for the National Anthem. Then get to work finding me a real catcher. If you want to have any chance at all of contending this season, that is." Then he hung up and lit what was probably his eightieth cigarette of the day.

Oh for the life of a manager, huh? One catcher facing manslaughter charges; another in the hospital, wrapped in so many bandages he looked like Boris Karloff in *The Mummy*; a pitching staff either not old enough to shave or about ready for the Sociable Security; God-knows-who about to put on the gear and squat behind the plate on Opening Day.

We flew north that year instead of riding the rails, but it still felt like a train wreck. Meanwhile, Kerwin McCaslin, who was the Titans' GM, got on the phone and found us a catcher to start the season with: William Blakely, soon to be known as Blockade Billy. I can't remember now if he came from Double or Triple A, but you could look it up on your computer, I guess, because I *do* know the name of the team he came from:

the Davenport Cornhuskers. A few players came up from there during my seven years with the Titans, and the regulars would always ask how things were down there playing for the Cornholers. Or sometimes they'd call them the Cocksuckers. Baseball humor is not what you'd call sophisticated.

We opened against the Red Sox that year. Middle of April. Baseball started later back then, and played a saner schedule. I got to the park early that day—before God got out of bed, actually—and there was a young man sitting on the bumper of an old Ford truck in the players' lot. Iowa license plate dangling on chicken-wire from the back bumper. Nick the guard let him in when the kid showed him his letter from the front office and his driver's license.

"You must be Bill Blakely," I said, shaking his hand. "Good to know you."

"Good to know you, too," he said. "I brought my gear, but it's pretty beat-up."

"Oh, I think we can take care of you there, part-ner," I said, letting go of his hand. He had a Band-Aid wrapped around his second finger, just below the middle knuckle. "Cut yourself shaving?" I asked, pointing to it.

"Yup, cut myself shaving," he says. I couldn't tell if that was his way of showing he got my little joke, or if he was so worried about fucking up he thought he ought to agree with everything anyone said, at least to begin with. Later on I realized it was neither of those things; he just had a habit of echoing back what you said to him. I got used to it, even sort of got to like it.

"Are you the manager?" he asked. "Mr. DiPunno?"

"No," I said, "I'm George Grantham. Granny to you. I coach third base. I'm also the equipment manager." Which was the truth; I did both jobs. Told you the game was smaller then. "I'll get you fixed up, don't worry. All new gear."

"All new gear," says he. "Except for the glove. I have to have Billy's old glove, you know. Billy Junior and me's been the miles."

"Well, that's fine with me." And we went on in to what the sports writers used to call Old Swampy in those days.

I hesitated over giving him 19, because it was poor

old Faraday's number, but the uniform fit him without looking like pajamas, so I did. While he was dressing, I said: "Ain't you tired? You must have driven
almost nonstop. Didn't they send you some cash to
take a plane?"

"I ain't tired," he said. "They might have sent me
some cash to take a plane, but I didn't see it. Could we
go look at the field?"

I said we could, and led him down the runway and
up through the dugout. He walked down to home
plate outside the foul line in Faraday's uniform, the
blue 19 gleaming in the morning sun (it wasn't but
eight o'clock, the groundskeepers just starting what
would be a long day's work).

I wish I could tell you how it felt to see him taking that walk, Mr. King, but words are your thing,
not mine. All I know is that back-to he looked more
like Faraday than ever. He was ten years younger, of
course . . . but age doesn't show much from the back,
except sometimes in a man's walk. Plus he was slim
like Faraday, and slim's the way you want your shortstop and second baseman to look, not your catcher.

Catchers should be built like fireplugs, the way Johnny Goodkind was. This one looked like a bunch of broken ribs waiting to happen.

He had a firmer build than Frank Faraday, though; broader butt and thicker thighs. He was skinny from the waist up, but looking at him ass-end-going-away, I remember thinking he looked like what he probably was: an Iowa plowboy on vacation in scenic Newark.

He went to the plate and turned around to look out to dead center. He had dark hair and a lock of it had fallen on his forehead. He brushed it away and just stood there taking it all in—the silent, empty stands where over fifty thousand people would be sitting that afternoon, the bunting already hung on the railings and fluttering in the little morning breeze, the foul poles painted fresh Jersey Blue, the groundskeepers just starting to water. It was an awesome sight, I always thought, and I could imagine what was going through the kid's mind, him that had probably been home milking the cows just a week ago and waiting for the Cornholers to start playing in mid-May.

Blockade Billy

I thought, *Poor kid's finally getting the picture. When he looks over here, I'll see the panic in his eyes. I may have to tie him down in the locker room to keep him from jumping in that old truck of his and hightailing it back to God's country.*

But when he looked at me, there was no panic in his eyes. No fear. Not even nervousness, which I would have said every player feels on Opening Day. No, he looked perfectly cool standing there behind the plate in his Levi's and light poplin jacket.

"Yuh," he says, like a man confirming something he was pretty sure of in the first place. "Billy can hit here."

"Good for him," I tells him. It's all I can think of to say.

"Good," he says back. Then—I swear—he says, "Do you think those guys need help with them hoses?"

I laughed. There was something strange about him, something off, something that made folks nervous . . . but that something made people take to him, too. Kinda sweet. Something that made you want to like him in spite of feeling he wasn't exactly right in the top story. Joe felt it right away. Some of the players did, too, but that didn't stop them from liking him. I don't know, it was like when you talked to him what came back was the sound of your own voice. Like an echo in a cave.

"Billy," I said, "groundskeeping ain't your job. Bill's job is to put on the gear and catch Danny Dusen this afternoon."

"Danny Doo," he said.

"That's right. Twenty and six last year, should have won the Cy Young, didn't. He's still got a red ass over that. And remember this: If he shakes you off, don't you dare flash the same sign again. Not unless you want your pecker and asshole to change places after the game, that is. Danny Doo is four games from two hundred wins, and he's going to be mean as hell until he gets there."

"Until he gets there." Nodding his head.

"That's right."

"If he shakes me off, flash something different."

"Yes."

"Does he have a changeup?"

"Do you have two legs? The Doo's won a hundred

and ninety-six games. You don't do that without a changeup."

"Not without a changeup," he says. "Okay."

"And don't get hurt out there. Until the front office can make a deal, you're what we got."

"I'm it," he says. "Gotcha."

"I hope so."

Other players were coming in by then, and I had about a thousand things to do. Later on I saw the kid in Jersey Joe's office, signing whatever needed to be signed with Kerwin McCaslin hanging over him like a vulture over roadkill, pointing out all the right places. Poor kid, probably six hours' worth of sleep in the last sixty, and he was in there signing five years of his life away. Later I saw him with Dusen, going over the Boston lineup. The Doo was doing all the talking, and the kid was doing all the listening. Didn't even ask a question, so far as I saw, which was good. If the kid had opened his head, Danny probably would have bit it off.

About an hour before the game, I went in to Joe's office to look at the lineup card. He had the kid batting eighth, which was no shock. Over our heads the murmuring had started and you could hear the rumble of feet on the boards. Opening Day crowds always pile in early. Listening to it started the butterflies in my gut, like always, and I could see Jersey Joe felt the same. His ashtray was already overflowing.

"He's not big like I hoped he'd be," he said, tapping Blakely's name on the lineup card. "God help us if he gets cleaned out."

"McCaslin hasn't found anyone else?"

"Maybe. He talked to Hubie Rattner's wife, but Hubie's on a fishing trip somewhere in Rectal Temperature, Michigan. Out of touch until next week."

"Cap—Hubie Rattner's forty-three if he's a day."

"Beggars can't be choosers. And be straight with me—how long do you think that kid's gonna last in the bigs?"

"Oh, he's probably just a cup of coffee," I says, "but he's got something Faraday didn't."

"And what might that be?"

"Dunno. But if you'd seen him standing behind the plate and looking out into center, you might feel bet-

ter about him. It was like he was thinking 'This ain't
the big deal I thought it would be.'"

"He'll find out how big a deal it is the first time Ike
Delock throws one at his nose," Joe said, and lit a cigarette. He took a drag and started hacking. "I got to
quit these Luckies. Not a cough in a carload, my ass.
I'll bet you twenty goddam bucks that kid lets Danny
Doo's first curve go right through his wickets. Then
Danny'll be all upset—you know how he gets when
someone fucks up his train ride—and Boston'll be off
to the races."

"Ain't you just the cheeriest Cheerio," I says.

He stuck out his hand. "Bet."

And because I knew he was trying to take the curse
off it, I shook his hand. That was twenty I won, because
the legend of Blockade Billy started that very day.

You couldn't say he called a good game, because he
didn't call it. The Doo did that. But the first pitch—
to Frank Malzone—*was* a curve, and the kid caught it
just fine. Not only that, though. It was a cunt's hair
outside and I never saw a catcher pull one back so fast,
not even Yogi. Ump called strike one and it was us off

to the races, at least until Williams hit a solo shot in the fifth. We got that back in the sixth, when Ben Vincent put one out. Then in the seventh, we've got a runner on second—I think it was Barbarino—with two outs and the new kid at the plate. It was his third at bat. First time he struck out looking, the second time swinging. Delock fooled him bad that time, made him look silly, and he heard the only boos he ever got while he was wearing a Titans uniform.

He steps in, and I looked over at Joe. Seen him sitting way down by the lineup card, just looking at the floor and shaking his head. Even if the kid worked a walk, The Doo was up next, and The Doo couldn't hit a slowpitch softball with a tennis racket. As a hitter that guy was fucking terrible.

I won't drag out the suspense; this ain't no kids' sports novel. Although whoever said life sometimes imitates art was right, and it did that day. Count went to three and two. Then Delock threw the sinker that fooled the kid so bad the first time and damn if the kid didn't suck for it again. Except Ike Delock turned out to be the sucker that time. Kid golfed it right off

20

his shoetops the way Ellie Howard used to do and shot it into the gap. I waved the runner in and we had the lead back, two to one.

Everybody in the joint was on their feet, screaming their throats out, but the kid didn't even seem to hear it. Just stood there on second, dusting off the seat of his pants. He didn't stay there long, because The Doo went down on three pitches, then threw his bat like he always did when he got struck out.

So maybe it's a sports novel after all, like the kind you probably read in junior high school study hall. Top of the ninth and The Doo's looking at the top of the lineup. Strikes out Malzone, and a quarter of the crowd's on their feet. Strikes out Klaus, and half the crowd's on their feet. Then comes Williams—old Teddy Ballgame. The Doo gets him on the hip, oh and two, then weakens and walks him. The kid starts out to the mound and Doo waves him back—just squat and do your job, sonny. So sonny does. What else is he gonna do? The guy on the mound is one of the best pitchers in baseball and the guy behind the plate was maybe playing a little pickup ball behind the barn that spring to keep in shape after the day's cowtits was all pulled.

First pitch, goddam! Williams takes off for second. The ball was in the dirt, hard to handle, but the kid still made one fuck of a good throw. Almost got Teddy, but as you know, almost only counts in horseshoes. Now everybody's on their feet, screaming. The Doo does some shouting at the kid—like it was the kid's fault instead of just a bullshit pitch—and while Doo's telling the kid he's a lousy choker, Williams calls time. Hurt his knee a little sliding into the bag, which shouldn't have surprised anyone; he could hit like nobody's business, but he was a leadfoot on the bases. Why he stole a bag that day is anybody's guess. It sure wasn't no hit-and-run, not with two outs and the game on the line.

So Billy Anderson comes in to run for Teddy . . . who probably would have been royally roasted by the manager if he'd been anyone but Teddy. And Dick Gernert steps in, .425 slugging percentage or something like it. The crowd's going apeshit, the flag's blowing out, the frank wrappers are swirling around, women are goddam crying, men are yelling for Jersey Joe to yank The Doo and put in Stew Rankin—he was what people would call the closer today, although back then he was just known as a short-relief specialist.

But Joe crossed his fingers and stuck with Dusen.

The count goes three and two, right? Anderson off with the pitch, right? Because he can run like the wind and the guy behind the plate's a first-game rook. Gernert, that mighty man, gets just under a curve and beeps it—not bloops it but *beeps* it—behind the pitcher's mound, just out of The Doo's reach. He's on it like a cat, though. Anderson's around third and The Doo throws home from his knees. That thing was a fucking *bullet*.

I know what you're thinking *I'm* thinking, Mr. King, but you're dead wrong. It never crossed my mind that our new rookie catcher was going to get busted up like Faraday and have a nice one-game career in the bigs. For one thing, Billy Anderson was no moose like Big Klew; more of a ballet dancer. For another . . . well . . . the kid was *better* than Faraday. I think I knew that the first time I saw him, sitting on the bumper of his beshitted old truck with his wore-out gear stored in the back.

Dusen's throw was low but on the money. The kid took it between his legs, then pivoted around, and I seen he was holding out *just the mitt*. I just had time to think of what a rookie mistake that was, how he forgot that old saying *two hands for beginners,* how Anderson was going to knock the ball loose and we'd have to try to win the game in the bottom of the ninth. But then the kid lowered his left shoulder like a football line-man. I never paid attention to his free hand, because I was staring at that outstretched catcher's mitt, just like everyone else in Old Swampy that day. So I didn't exactly see what happened, and neither did anybody else.

What I *saw* was this: The kid whapped the glove on Anderson's chest while he was still three full steps from the dish. Then Anderson hit the kid's lowered shoulder. He went up and over and landed behind the lefthand batter's box. The umpire lifted his fist in the *out* sign. Then Anderson started to yell and grab his ankle. I could hear it from the far end of the dugout, so you know it must have been good yelling, because those Opening Day fans were roaring like a force-ten gale. I could see that Anderson's left pants cuff was turning red, and blood was oozing out between his fingers.

Can I have a drink of water? Just pour some out of that plastic pitcher, would you? Plastic pitchers is all they give us for our rooms, you know; no glass pitchers allowed in the zombie hotel.

Ah, that's good. Been a long time since I talked so much, and I got a lot more to say. You bored yet? No? Good. Me neither. Having the time of my life, awful story or not.

Anderson didn't play again until '58, and '58 was his last year—Boston gave him his unconditional release halfway through the season, and he couldn't catch on with anyone else. Because his speed was gone, and speed was really all he had to sell. The docs said he'd be good as new, the Achilles tendon was only nicked, not cut all the way through, but it was also stretched, and I imagine that's what finished him. Baseball's a tender game, you know; people don't realize. And it isn't only catchers who get hurt in collisions at the plate.

After the game, Danny Doo grabs the kid in the shower and yells: "I'm gonna buy you a drink tonight, rook! In fact, I'm gonna buy you *ten*!" And then he gives his highest praise: "*You hung the fuck in there!*"

"Ten drinks, because I hung the fuck in there," the kid says, and The Doo laughs and claps him on the back like it's the funniest thing he ever heard.

But then Pinky Higgins comes storming in. He was managing the Red Sox that year, which was a thankless job; things only got worse for Pinky and the Sox as the summer of '57 crawled along. He was mad as hell, chewing a wad of tobacco so hard and fast the juice squirted from both sides of his mouth and ran down his chin. He said the kid had deliberately cut Anderson's ankle when they collided at the plate. Said Blakely must have done it with his fingernails, and the kid should be put out of the game for it. This was pretty rich, coming from a man whose motto was, "Spikes high and let em die!"

I was sitting in Joe's office drinking a beer, so the

two of us listened to Pinky's rant together. I thought the guy was nuts, and I could see from Joe's face that I wasn't alone.

Joe waited until Pinky ran down, then said: "I wasn't watching Anderson's foot. I was watching to see if Blakely made the tag and held on to the ball. Which he did."

"Get him in here," Pinky fumes. "I want to say it to his face."

"Be reasonable, Pink," Joe says. "Would I be in your office doing a tantrum if it had been Blakely all cut up?"

"It wasn't spikes!" Pinky yells. "Spikes are a part of the game! Scratching someone up like a . . . a girl at a *kickball match* . . . that *ain't*! And Anderson's in the game seven years! He's got a family to support!"

"So you're saying what? My catcher ripped your pinch-runner's ankle open while he was tagging him out—and tossing him over his goddam shoulder, don't forget—and he did it with his *nails*?"

"That's what Anderson says," Pinky tells him. "Anderson says he felt it."

"Maybe Blakely stretched Anderson's foot with his nails, too. Is that it?"

"No," Pinky admits. His face was all red by then, and not just from being mad. He knew how it sounded. "He says that happened when he came down."

"Begging the court's pardon," I says, "but *fingernails*? This is a load of crap."

"I want to see the kid's hands," Pinky says. "You show me or I'll lodge a goddam protest."

I thought Joe would tell Pinky to shit in his hat, but he didn't. He turned to me. "Tell the kid to come in here. Tell him he's gonna show Mr. Higgins his nails, just like he did to his first-grade teacher after the Pledge of Alliegence."

I got the kid. He came willingly enough, although he was just wearing a towel, and didn't hold back showing his nails. They were short, clean, not broken, not even bent. There were no blood-blisters, either, like there might be if you really set them in someone and raked with them. One little thing I did happen to notice, although I didn't think anything of it at the time: The Band-Aid was gone from his second finger, and I didn't see any sign of a healing cut where it had been, just clean skin, pink from the shower.

"Satisfied?" Joe asked Pinky. "Or would you like to check his ears for potato-dirt while you're at it?"

"Fuck you," Pinky says. He got up, stamped over to the door, spat his cud into the wastepaper basket there—*splut!*—and then he turns back. "My boy says *your* boy cut him. Says he felt it. And my boy don't lie."

"Your boy tried to be a hero with the game on the line instead of stopping at third and giving Piersall a chance. He'd tell you the moon was made of his father's come-stained skivvies if it'd get him off the hook for that. You know what happened and so do I. Anderson got tangled in his own spikes and did it to himself when he went whoopsy-daisy. Now get out of here."

"There'll be a payback for this, DiPunno."

"Yeah? Well it's the same gametime tomorrow. Get here early."

Pinky left, already tearing off a fresh piece of chew. Joe drummed his fingers beside his ashtray, then asked the kid: "Now that it's just us chickens, did you do anything to Anderson? Tell me the truth."

29

"No." Not a bit of hesitation. "I didn't do anything to Anderson. That's the truth."

"Okay," Joe said, and stood up. "Always nice to shoot the shit after a game, but I think I'll go on home and have a drink. Then I might fuck my wife on the sofa. Winning on Opening Day always makes my pecker stand up." Then he said, "Kid, you played the game the way it's supposed to be played. Good for you."

He left. The kid cinched his towel around his waist and started back to the locker room. I said, "I see that shaving cut's all better."

He stopped dead in the doorway, and although his back was to me, I knew he'd done something out there. The truth was in the way he was standing. I don't know how to explain it better, but . . . I knew.

"What?" Like he didn't get me, you know.

"The shaving cut on your finger."

"Oh, *that* shaving cut. Yuh, all better."

And out he sails . . . although, rube that he was, he probably didn't have a clue *where* he was going. Luckily for him, Kerwin McCaslin had got him a place to stay in the better part of Newark. Hard to believe as it might be, Newark had a better part back then.

Okay, second game of the season. Dandy Dave Sisler on the mound for Boston, and our new catcher is hardly settled into the batter's box before Sisler chucks a fastball at his head. Would have knocked his fucking eyes out if it had connected, but he snaps his head back—didn't duck or nothing—and then just cocks his bat again, looking at Sisler as if to say, *Go on, mac, do it again if you want.*

The crowd's screaming like mad and chanting *RUN IM! RUN IM! RUN IM!* The ump didn't run Sisler, but he got warned and a cheer went up. I looked over and saw Pinky in the Boston dugout, walking back and forth with his arms folded so tight he looked like he was trying to keep from exploding.

Sisler walks twice around the mound, soaking up the fan-love—boy oh boy, they wanted him drawn and quartered—and then he went to the rosin bag, and then he shook off two or three signs. Taking his time, you know, letting it sink in. The kid all the time just standing there with his bat cocked, comfortable as old

Tillie. So Dandy Dave throws a get-me-over fastball right down Broadway and the kid loses it in the left field bleachers. Tidings was on base and we're up two to nothing. I bet the people over in New York heard the noise from Swampy when the kid hit that home run.

I thought he'd be grinning when he came around third, but he looked just as serious as a judge. Under his breath he's muttering, "Got it done, Billy, showed that busher and got it done."

The Doo was the first one to grab him in the dug-out and danced him right into the bat-rack. Helped him pick up the spilled lumber, too, which was noth-ing like Danny Dusen, who usually thought he was above such things.

After beating Boston twice and pissing off Pinky Higgins, we went down to Washington and won three straight. The kid hit safe in all three, including his sec-ond home run, but Griffith Stadium was a depressing place to play, brother; you could have gunned down a running rat in the box seats behind home plate and not had to worry about hitting any fans. Goddam Senators finished over forty games back that year. Forty! Jesus fucking wept.

The kid was behind the plate for The Doo's second start down there and damn near caught a no-hitter in his fifth game wearing a big-league uniform. Pete Runnels spoiled it in the ninth—hit a double with one out. After that, the kid went out to the mound, and that time Danny didn't wave him back. They discussed it a little bit, and then The Doo gave an intentional pass to the next batter, Lou Berberet (see how it all comes back?). That brought up Bob Usher, and he hit into a double play just as sweet as you could ever want: ballgame.

That night The Doo and the kid went out to celebrate Dusen's one hundred and ninety-eighth win. When I saw our newest chick the next day, he was very badly hungover, but he bore that as calmly as he bore having Dave Sisler chuck at his head. I was starting to think we had a real big leaguer on our hands, and wouldn't be needing Hubie Rattner after all. Or anybody else.

"You and Danny are getting pretty tight, I guess," I says.

"Tight," he agrees, rubbing his temples. "Me and The Doo are tight. He says Billy's his good luck charm."

"Does he, now?"

"Yuh. He says if we stick together, he'll win twenty-five and they'll have to give him the Cy Young."

"That right?"

"Yessir, that's right. Granny?"

"What?"

He was giving me that wide blue stare of his: twenty-twenty vision that saw everything and understood practically nothing. By then I knew he could hardly read, and the only movie he'd ever seen was *Bambi*. He said he went with the other kids from Ottershow or Outershow—whatever—and I assumed it was his school. I was both right and wrong about that, but it ain't really the point. The point is that he knew how to play baseball—instinctively, I'd say—but otherwise he was a blackboard with nothing written on it.

"What's a Cy Young?"

That's how he was, you see.

We went over to Baltimore for three before going

back home. Typical spring baseball in that town, which isn't quite south or north; cold enough to freeze the balls off a brass monkey the first day, hotter than hell the second, a fine drizzle like liquid ice the third. Didn't matter to the kid; he hit in all three games, making it eight straight. Also, he stopped another runner at the plate. We lost the game, but it was a hell of a stop. Gus Triandos was the victim, I think. He ran headfirst into the kid's knees and just lay there stunned, three feet from home. The kid put the tag on the back of his neck just as gentle as Mommy patting oil on Baby Dear's sunburn.

There was a picture of that putout in the Newark *Evening News,* with a caption reading *Blockade Billy Blakely Saves Another Run.* It was a good nickname and caught on with the fans. They weren't as demonstrative in those days—nobody would have come to Yankee Stadium in '57 wearing a chef's hat to support Garry Sheffield, I don't think—but when we played our first game back at Old Swampy, some of the fans came in carrying orange road-signs reading DETOUR and ROAD CLOSED.

The signs might have been a one-day thing if two Indians hadn't got thrown out at the plate in our first game back. That was a game Danny Dusen pitched, incidentally. Both of those putouts were the result of great throws rather than great blocks, but the rook got the credit, anyway, and I'd say he deserved it. The guys were starting to trust him, see? And they wanted to watch him do it. Baseball players are fans, too, and when someone's on a roll, even the most hard-hearted try to help.

Dusen got his hundred and ninety-ninth that day. Oh, and the kid went three for four, including a home run, so it shouldn't surprise you that even more people showed up with those signs for our second game against Cleveland.

By the third one, some enterprising fellow was selling them out on Titan Esplanade, big orange cardboard diamonds with black letters: ROAD CLOSED BY ORDER OF BLOCKADE BILLY. Some of the fans'd hold em up when Blockade Billy was at bat, and they'd all hold them up when the other team had a runner on third. By the time the Yankees came to town—this was going on to the end of April—the whole stadium would flush orange when the Bombers had a runner on third, which they did often in that series.

Because the Yankees kicked the living shit out of us and took over first place. It was no fault of the kid's; he hit in every game and tagged out Bill Skowron between home and third when the lug got caught in a rundown. Skowron was a moose the size of Big Klew, and he tried to flatten the kid, but it was Skowron who went on his ass, the kid straddling him with a knee on either side. The photo of that one in the paper made it look like the end of a Big Time Wrestling match with Pretty Tony Baba for once finishing off Gorgeous George instead of the other way around. The crowd outdid themselves waving those ROAD CLOSED signs around. It didn't seem to matter that the Titans had lost; the fans went home happy because they'd seen our skinny catcher knock Mighty Moose Skowron on his ass.

I seen the kid afterward, sitting naked on the bench outside the showers. He had a big bruise coming on the side of his chest, but he didn't seem to mind it

37

at all. He was no crybaby. The sonofabitch was too dumb to feel pain, some people said later; too dumb and crazy. But I've known plenty of dumb players in my time, and being dumb never stopped them from bitching over their booboos.

"How about all those signs, kid?" I asked, thinking I would cheer him up if he needed cheering.

"What signs?" he says, and I could see by the puzzled look on his face that he wasn't joking a bit. That was Blockade Billy for you. He would have stood in front of a semi if the guy behind the wheel was driving down the third baseline and trying to score on him, but otherwise he didn't have a fucking clue.

We played a two-game series with Detroit before hitting the road again, and lost both. Danny Doo was on the mound for the second one, and he couldn't blame the kid for the way it went; he was gone before the third inning was over. Sat in the dugout whining about the cold weather (it wasn't cold), the way Harrington misplayed a fly ball out in right (Harrington would have needed rockets on his heels to get to that one before it dropped), and the bad calls he got from

38

that sonofabitch Wenders behind the plate. On that last one he might have had a point. Hi Wenders didn't like The Doo, never had, ran him in two ballgames the year before. But I didn't see any bad calls that day, and I was standing less than ninety feet away.

The kid hit safe in both games, including a home run and a triple. Nor did Dusen hold the hot bat against him, which would have been his ordinary behavior; he was one of those guys who wanted fellows to understand there was one big star on the Titans, and it wasn't them. But he liked the kid; really seemed to think the kid was his lucky charm. And the kid liked him. They went bar-hopping after the game, had about a thousand drinks and visited a whorehouse to celebrate The Doo's first loss of the season, and showed up the next day for the trip to KC pale and shaky.

"The kid got laid last night," Doo confided in me as we rode out to the airport in the team bus. "I think it was his first time. That's the good news. The bad news is that I don't think he remembers it."

We had a bumpy plane-ride; most of them were back then. Lousy prop-driven buckets, it's a wonder we didn't all get killed like Buddy Holly and the Big Fucking Bopper. The kid spent most of the trip throwing up in the can at the back of the plane, while right outside the door a bunch of guys sat playing acey-deucey and tossing him the usual funny stuff: *Get any onya? Want a fork and knife to cut that up a little?* Then the next day the sonofabitch goes five-for-five at Municipal Stadium, including a pair of jacks.

There was also another Blockade Billy play; by then he could have taken out a patent. This time the victim was Clete Boyer. Again it was Blockade Billy down with the left shoulder, and up and over Mr. Boyer went, landing flat on his back in the left batter's box. There were some differences, though. The rook used both hands on the tag, and there was no bloody foot or strained Achilles tendon. Boyer just got up and walked back to the dugout, dusting his ass and shaking his head like he didn't quite know where he was. Oh, and we lost the game in spite of the kid's five hits. Eleven to ten was the final score, or something like that. Ganzie Burgess's knuckleball wasn't dancing that day; the Athletics feasted on it.

Blockade Billy

We won the next game, lost a squeaker on getaway day. The kid hit in both games, which made it sixteen straight. Plus nine putouts at the plate. Nine in sixteen games! That might be a record. If it was in the books, that is. If any of that month's records were in the books.

We went to Chicago for three, and the kid hit in those games, too, making it nineteen straight. But damn if we didn't lose all three. Jersey Joe looked at me after the last of those games and said, "I don't buy that lucky charm stuff. I think Blakely *sucks* luck."

"That ain't fair and you know it," I said. "We were going good at the start, and now we're in a bad patch. It'll even out."

"Maybe," he says. "Is Dusen still trying to teach the kid how to drink?"

"Yeah. They headed off to The Loop with some other guys."

"But they'll come back together," Joe says. "I don't get it. By now Dusen should hate that kid. Doo's been here five years and I know his MO."

I did, too. When The Doo lost, he had to lay the

41

blame on somebody else, like that bum Johnny Harrington or that busher bluesuit Hi Wenders. The kid's turn in the barrel was overdue, but Danny was still clapping him on the back and promising him he'd be Rookie of the Goddam Year. Not that The Doo could blame the kid for that day's loss. In the fifth inning of his latest masterpiece, Danny had hucked one to the backstop in the fifth: high, wide, and handsome. That scored one. So then he gets mad, loses his control, and walks the next two. Then Nellie Fox doubled down the line. After that The Doo got it back together, but by then it was too late; he was on the hook and stayed there.

We got a little well in Detroit, took two out of three. The kid hit in all three games and made another one of those amazing home-plate stands. Then we flew home. By then the kid from the Davenport Cornholers was the hottest goddam thing in the American League. There was talk of him doing a Gillette ad.

"That's an ad I'd like to see," Si Barbarino said. "I'm a fan of comedy."

"Then you must love looking at yourself in the mirror," Critter Hayward said.

"You're a card," Si says. "What I mean is the kid ain't got no whiskers."

There never was an ad, of course. Blockade Billy's career as a baseball player was almost over. We just didn't know it.

We had three scheduled at home with the White Sox, but the first one was a washout. The Doo's old pal Hi Wenders was the umpire crew chief, and he gave me the news himself. I'd got to The Swamp early because the trunks with our road uniforms in them got sent to Idlewild by mistake and I wanted to make sure they'd been trucked over. We wouldn't need them for a week, but I was never easy in my mind until such things were taken care of.

Wenders was sitting on a little stool outside the umpire's room, reading a paperback with a blond in step-ins on the cover.

"That your wife, Hi?" I asks.

"My girlfriend," he says. "Go on home, Granny. Weather forecast says that by three it's gonna be coming down in buckets. I'm just waiting for DiPunno and Lopez to get here so I can call the game."

"Okay," I says. "Thanks." I started away and he called after me.

"Granny, is that wonder-kid of yours all right in the head? Because he talks to himself behind the plate. Whispers. Never fucking shuts up."

"He's no Quiz Kid, but he's not crazy, if that's what you mean," I said. I was wrong about that, but who knew? "What kind of stuff does he say?"

"I couldn't hear much the one time I was behind him—the second game against Boston—but I know he talks about himself. In that whatdoyoucallit, third person. He says stuff like 'I can do it, Billy.' And one time, when he dropped a foul tip that woulda been strike three, he goes, 'I'm sorry, Billy.'"

"Well, so what? Til I was five, I had an invisible friend named Sheriff Pete. Me and Sheriff Pete shot up a lot of mining towns together."

"Yeah, but Blakely ain't five anymore. Unless he's five up here." Wenders taps the side of his thick skull.

"He's apt to have a five as the first number in his batting average before long," I says. "That's all I care about. Plus he's a hell of a stopper. You have to admit that."

"I do," Wenders says. "That little cock-knocker has no fear. Another sign that he's not all there in the head."

I wasn't going to listen to an umpire run down one of my players any more than that, so I changed the subject and asked him—joking but not joking—if he was going to call the game tomorrow fair and square, even though his favorite Doo-Bug was throwing.

"I always call it fair and square," he says. "Dusen's a conceited glory-hog who's got his spot all picked out in Cooperstown, he'll do a hundred things wrong and never take the blame once, and he's an argumentative sonofabitch who knows better than to start in with me, because I won't stand for it. That said, I'll call it straight-up, just like I always do. I can't believe you'd ask."

And I can't believe you'd sit there scratching your ass and calling our catcher next door to a congenital idiot, I thought, *but you did.*

I took my wife out to dinner that night, and we had a very nice time. Danced to Lester Lanin's band, as I recall. Got a little romantic in the taxi afterward. Slept well. I didn't sleep well for quite some time afterward; lots of bad dreams.

Danny Dusen took the ball in what was supposed to be the afternoon half of a twi-nighter, but the world as it applied to the Titans had already gone to hell; we just didn't know it. No one did except for Joe DiPunno. By the time night fell, we knew we were fucked for the season, because our first twenty-two games were almost surely going to be erased from the record books, along with any official acknowledgment of Blockade Billy Blakely.

I got in late because of traffic, but figured it didn't matter because the uniform snafu was sorted out. Most of the guys were already there, dressing or playing poker or just sitting around shooting the shit. Dusen and the kid were over in the corner by the cigarette machine, sitting in a couple of folding chairs, the kid with his uniform pants on, Dusen still wearing nothing but his jock—not a pretty sight. I went over to get a pack of Winstons and listened in. Danny was doing most of the talking.

"That fucking Wenders hates my ass," he says.

"He hates your ass," the kid says, then adds: "That fucker."

46

"You bet he is. You think he wants to be the one behind the plate when I get my two hundredth?"

"No?" the kid says.

"You bet he don't! But I'm going to win today just to spite him. And you're gonna help me, Bill. Right?"

"Right. Sure. Bill's gonna help."

"He'll squeeze like a motherfucker."

"Will he? Will he squeeze like a motherf—"

"I just said he will. So you pull everything back."

"I'll pull everything back."

"You're my good luck charm, Billy-boy."

And the kid, grinning: "I'm your good luck charm."

"Yeah. Now listen . . ."

It was funny and creepy at the same time. The Doo was *intense*—leaning forward, eyes flashing while he talked. Everything Wenders had said about him was true, but he left one thing out: The Doo was a competitor. He wanted to win the way Bob Gibson did. Like Gibby, he'd do anything he could get away with to make that happen. And the kid was eating it up with a spoon.

I almost said something, because I wanted to break

up that connection. Talking about it to you, I think maybe my subconscious mind had already put a lot of it together. Maybe that's bullshit, but I don't think so.

In any case, I left them alone, just got my butts and walked away. Hell, if I'd opened my bazoo, Dusen would have told me to put a sock in it, anyway. He didn't like to be interrupted when he was holding court, and while I might not have given much of a shit about that on any other day, you tend to leave a guy alone when it's his turn to toe the rubber in front of the forty thousand people who are paying his salary. Especially when he's up for the big two-double-zero.

I went over to Joe's office to get the lineup card, but the office door was shut and the blinds were down, an almost unheard-of thing on a game day. The slats weren't closed, so I peeked through. Joe had the phone to his ear and one hand over his eyes. I knocked on the glass. He started so hard he almost fell out of his chair, then looked around. And I saw he was crying. I never saw him cry in my life, not before or after, but he was crying that day. His face was pale and his hair was wild—what little hair he had.

Blockade Billy

He waved me away, then went back to talking on the phone. I started across the locker room to the coaches' office, which was really the equipment room. Halfway there I stopped. The big pitcher-catcher conference had broken up, and the kid was pulling on his uniform shirt, the one with the big blue 19. And I saw the Band-Aid was back on the second finger of his right hand.

I walked over and put a hand on his shoulder. He smiled at me. The kid had a real sweet smile when he used it. "Hi, Granny," he says. But his smile began to fade when he saw I wasn't smiling back.

"You all ready to play?" I asked.

"Sure."

"Good. But I want to tell you something first. The Doo's a hell of a pitcher, but as a human being he ain't ever going to get past Double A. He'd walk on his grandmother's broken back to get a win, and you matter a hell of a lot less to him than his grandmother."

"I'm his good luck charm!" he says indignantly . . . but underneath the indignation, he looked ready to cry.

"Maybe so," I said, "but that's not what I'm talking

about. There's such a thing as getting *too* pumped up for a game. A little is good, but too much and a fellow's apt to bust wide open."

"I don't get you."

"If you popped and went flat like a bad tire, The Doo wouldn't give much of a shit. He'd just find himself a brand-new lucky charm."

"You shouldn't talk like that! Him and me's friends!"

"I'm your friend, too. More important, I'm one of the coaches on this team. I'm responsible for your welfare, and I'll talk any goddam way I want, especially to a rook. And you'll listen. Are you listening?"

"I'm listening."

I'm sure he was, but he wasn't looking; he'd cast his eyes down and sullen red roses were blooming on those smooth little-boy cheeks of his.

"I don't know what kind of a rig you've got under that Band-Aid, and I don't want to know. All I know is I saw it in the first game you played for us, and somebody got hurt. I haven't seen it since, and I don't want to see it today. Because if you got caught, it'd be *you* caught. Not The Doo."

"I just cut myself," he says, all sullen.

"Right. Shaving. But I don't want to see it on your finger when you go out there. I'm looking after your own best interests."

Would I have said that if I hadn't seen Joe so upset he was crying? I like to think so. I like to think I was also looking after the best interests of the game, which I loved then and now. Virtual Bowling can't hold a candle, believe me.

I walked away before he could say anything else. And I didn't look back. Partly because I didn't want to see what was under the Band-Aid, mostly because Joe was standing in his office door, beckoning to me. I won't swear there was more gray in his hair, but I won't swear there wasn't.

I came into the office and closed the door. An awful idea occurred to me. It made a kind of sense, given the look on his face. "Jesus, Joe, is it your wife? Or the kids? Did something happen to one of the kids?"

He started, like I'd just woken him out of a dream. "Jessie and the kids are fine. But George . . . oh *God*. I can't believe it. This is such a mess." And he put the heels of his palms against his eyes. A sound came out of him, but it wasn't a sob. It was a laugh. The most terrible fucked-up laugh I ever heard.

"What is it? Who called you?"

"I have to think," he says—but not to me. It was himself he was talking to. "I have to decide how I'm going to . . ." He took his hands off his eyes, and he seemed a little more like himself. "You're managing today, Granny."

"*Me?* I can't manage! The Doo'd blow his stack! He's going for his two hundredth again, and—"

"None of that matters, don't you see? Not now."

"What—"

"Just shut up and make out a lineup card. As for that kid . . ." He thought, then shook his head. "Hell, let him play, why not? Shit, bat him fifth. I was gonna move him up, anyway."

"Of course he's gonna play," I said. "Who else'd catch Danny?"

"Oh, fuck Danny Dusen!" he says.

"Cap—Joey—tell me what happened."

"No," he says. "I got to think about it first. What

52

I'm going to say to the guys. And the reporters!" He slapped his brow as if this part of it had just occurred to him. "*Those* overbred assholes! Shit!" Then, talking to himself again: "But let the guys have this game. They deserve that much. Maybe the kid, too. Hell, maybe he'll bat for the cycle!" He laughed some more, then went upside his own head to make himself stop.

"I don't understand."

"You will. Go on, get out of here. Make any old lineup you want. Pull the names out of a hat, why don't you? It doesn't matter. Only make sure you tell the umpire crew chief you're running the show. I guess that'd be Wenders."

I walked down the hall to the umpire's room like a man in a dream and told Wenders that I'd be making out the lineup and managing the game from the third base box. He asked me what was wrong with Joe, and I said Joe was sick.

That was the first game I managed until I got the Athletics in '63, and it was a short one, because as you probably know if you've done your research, Hi Wenders ran me in the sixth. I don't remember much about it, anyway. I had so much on my mind that I felt like a man in a dream. But I did have sense enough to do one thing, and that was to check the kid's right hand before he ran out on the field. There was no Band-Aid on the second finger, and no cut, either. I didn't even feel relieved. I just kept seeing Joe DiPunno's red eyes and haggard mouth.

That was Danny Doo's last good game ever, and he never did get his two hundred. He tried to come back in '58, but it was no good. He claimed the double vision was gone and maybe it was true, but he couldn't hardly get the pill over the plate anymore. No spot in Cooperstown for Danny. Joe was right: That kid did suck luck.

But that afternoon Doo was the best I ever saw him, his fastball hopping, his curve snapping like a whip. For the first four innings they couldn't touch him at all. Just wave the stick and take a seat, fellows. He struck out six and the rest were infield groundouts. Only trouble was, Kinder was almost as good. We'd gotten one lousy hit, a two-out double by Harrington in the bottom of the third.

Blockade Billy

Now it's the top of the fifth. The first batter goes down easy. Then Walt Dropo comes up, hits one deep into the left field corner, and takes off like a bat out of hell. The crowd saw Harry Keene still chasing the ball while Dropo's legging for second, and they understood it could be an inside-the-park job. The chanting started. Only a few voices at first, then more and more. Getting deeper and louder. It put a chill up me from the crack of my ass to the nape of my neck.

"Bloh-KADE! Bloh-KADE! Bloh-KADE!"

Like that. The orange signs started going up. People were on their feet and holding them over their heads. Not waving them like usual, just holding them up. I have never seen anything like it.

"Bloh-KADE! Bloh-KADE! Bloh-KADE!"

At first I thought there wasn't a snowball's chance in hell; by then Dropo's steaming for third with all the stops pulled out. But Keene pounced on the ball and made a perfect throw to Barbarino at short. The rook, meanwhile, is standing on the third-base side of home plate with his glove held out, making a target, and Si hit the goddam pocket.

55

The crowd's chanting. Dropo's sliding, spikes up. The kid don't mind; he goes on his knees and dives over em. Hi Wenders was where he was supposed to be—that time, at least—leaning over the play. A cloud of dust goes up . . . and out of it comes Wenders's upraised thumb. "*Yerrrr . . . OUT!*" Mr. King, the fans went nuts. Walt Dropo did, too. He was up and dancing around like a coked-up kid at a record hop. He couldn't believe it.

The kid was scraped halfway up his left forearm, not bad, just bloodsweat, but enough for old Bony Dadier—he was our trainer—to come out and slap a Band-Aid on it. So the kid got his Band-Aid after all, only this one was legit. The fans stayed on their feet during the whole medical consultation, waving their ROAD CLOSED signs and chanting "*Bloh-KADE! Bloh-KADE!*" like they wouldn't ever get enough of it.

The kid didn't seem to notice. He was in another world. He was the whole time he was with the Titans, now that I think of it. He just put on his mask, went back behind the plate, and squatted down. Business as usual. Bubba Phillips came up, lined out to Lathrop at first, and that was the fifth.

When the kid came up in the bottom of the inning and struck out on three pitches, the crowd still gave him a standing O. That time he noticed, and tipped his cap when he went back to the dugout. Only time he ever did it. Not because he was snotty but because . . . well, I already said it. That other world thing.

Okay, top of the sixth. Over fifty years later and I still get a red ass when I think of it. Kinder's up first and loops out to third, just like a pitcher should. Then comes Luis Aparicio, Little Louie. The Doo winds and fires. Aparicio fouls it off high and lazy behind home plate, on the third-base side of the screen. The kid throws away his mask and sprints after it, head back and glove out. Wenders trailed him, but not close like he should have done. He didn't think the kid had a chance. It was lousy goddam umping.

The kid's off the grass and on the track, by the low wall between the field and the box seats. Neck craned. Looking up. Two dozen people in those first- and second-row box seats also looking up, most of them waving their hands in the air. This is one thing I don't understand about fans and never will. It's a fucking *baseball,* for the love of God! An item that sold for seventy-five cents back then. Everybody knew it. But when fans see one in reach at the ballpark, they turn into fucking Danny Doo in order to get their hands on it. Never mind standing back and letting the man trying to catch it—*their* man, and in a tight ballgame—do his job.

I saw it all. Saw it clear. That mile-high popup came down on our side of the wall. The kid was going to catch it. Then some long-armed bozo in one of those Titans jerseys they sold on the Esplanade reached over and ticked it so the ball bounced off the edge of the kid's glove and fell to the ground.

I was so sure Wenders would call Aparacio out—it was clear interference—that at first I couldn't believe what I was seeing when he gestured for the kid to go back behind the plate and for Aparicio to resume the box. When I got it, I ran out, waving my arms. The crowd started cheering me and booing Wenders, which is no way to win friends and influence people

58

when you're arguing a call, but I was too goddam mad to care. I wouldn't have stopped if Mahatma Gandhi had walked out on the field butt-naked and urging us to make peace.

"*Interference!*" I yelled. "*Clear as day, clear as the nose on your face!*"

"It was in the stands, and that makes it anyone's ball," Wenders says. "Go on back to your little nest and let's get this show on the road."

The kid didn't care; he was talking to his pal The Doo. That was all right. I didn't care that he didn't care. All I wanted at that moment was to tear Hi Wenders a fresh new asshole. I'm not ordinarily an argumentative man—all the years I managed the A's, I only got thrown out of games twice—but that day I would have made Billy Martin look like a peacenik.

"*You didn't see it, Hi! You were trailing too far back! You didn't see shit!*"

"I wasn't trailing and I saw it all. Now get back, Granny. I ain't kidding."

"*If you didn't see that long-armed sonofabitch—*" (Here a lady in the second row put her hands over her lit-

59

tle boy's ears and pursed up her mouth at me in an oh-you-nasty-man look.) "—*that long-armed sonofabitch reach out and tick that ball, you were goddam trailing! Jesus Christ!*"

The man in the jersey starts shaking his head—who, me? not me!—but he's also wearing a big embarrassed suckass grin. Wenders saw it, knew what it meant, then looked away. "That's it," he says to me. And in the reasonable voice that means you're one smart crack from drinking a Rheingold in the locker room. "You've had your say. Now you can either go back to the dugout or you can listen to the rest of the game on the radio. Take your pick."

I went back to the dugout. Aparicio stood back in with a big shit-eating grin on his face. He knew, sure he did. And made the most of it. The guy never hit many home runs, but when The Doo sent in a change-up that didn't change, Louie cranked it high, wide, and handsome to the deepest part of the park. Nosy Norton was playing center, and he never even turned around.

Aparicio circled the bases, serene as the *Queen Mary*

coming into dock, while the crowd screamed at him, denigrated his relatives, and hurled hate down on Hi Wenders's head. Wenders heard none of it, which is the chief umpirely skill. He just got a fresh ball out of his coat pocket and inspected it for dings and doinks. Watching him do that, I lost it entirely. I rushed out to home plate and started shaking both fists in his face.

"That's your run, you fucking busher!" I screamed. *"Too fucking lazy to chase after a foul ball, and now you've got an RBI for yourself! Jam it up your ass! Maybe you'll find your glasses!"*

The crowd loved it. Hi Wenders, not so much. He pointed at me, threw his thumb back over his shoulder, and walked away. The crowd started booing and shaking their ROAD CLOSED signs; some threw bottles, cups, and half-eaten franks onto the field. It was a circus.

"Don't you walk away from me, you fatass blind lazy sonofabitching bastard!" I screamed, and chased after him. Someone from our dugout grabbed me before I could grab Wenders, which I meant to do. I had lost touch with reality.

The crowd was chanting *"KILL THE UMP! KILL THE UMP! KILL THE UMP!"* I'll never forget that, because it was the same way they'd been chanting *"Bloh-KADE! Bloh-KADE!"*

"If your mother was here, she'd be throwing shit at you, too, you bat-blind busher!" I screamed, and then they hauled me into the dugout. Ganzie Burgess, our knuckleballer, managed the last three innings of that horror-show. He also pitched the last two. You might find that in the record books, too. If there were any records of that lost spring.

The last thing I saw on the field was Danny Dusen and Blockade Billy standing on the grass between the plate and the mound. The kid had his mask tucked under his arm. The Doo was whispering in his ear. The kid was listening—he always listened when The Doo talked—but he was looking at the crowd, forty thousand fans on their feet, men, women, and children, yelling *KILL THE UMP, KILL THE UMP, KILL THE UMP.*

There was a bucket of balls halfway down the hall between the dugout and the locker room. I kicked it and sent balls rolling every whichway. If I'd stepped on one of them and fallen on my ass, it would have been the perfect end to a perfect fucking afternoon at the ballpark.

Joe was in the locker room, sitting on a bench outside the showers. By then he looked seventy instead of just fifty. There were three other guys in there with him. Two were uniformed cops. The third one was in a suit, but you only had to take one look at his hard roast beef of a face to know he was a cop, too.

"Game over early?" this one asked me. He was sitting on a folding chair with his big old cop thighs spread and straining his seersucker pants. The blue-suits were on one of the benches in front of the lockers.

"It is for me," I said. I was still so mad I didn't even care about the cops. To Joe I said, "Fucking Wenders ran me. I'm sorry, Cap, but it was a clear case of interference and that lazy sonofabitch—"

"It doesn't matter," Joe said. "The game isn't going to count. I don't think any of our games are going to count. Kerwin'll appeal to the Commissioner, of course, but—"

"What are you talking about?" I asked.

Joe sighed. Then he looked at the guy in the suit. "You tell him, Detective Lombardazzi," he said. "I can't bear to."

"Does he need to know?" Lombardazzi asked. He's looking at me like I'm some kind of bug he's never seen before. It was a look I didn't need on top of everything else, but I kept my mouth shut. Because I knew three cops, one of them a detective, don't show up in the locker room of a Major League baseball team if it isn't goddam serious.

"If you want him to hold the other guys long enough for you to get the Blakely kid out of here, I think he does need to," Joe says.

From above us there came a cry from the fans, followed by a groan, followed by a cheer. None of us paid any attention to what turned out to be the end of Danny Dusen's baseball career. The cry was when he got hit in the forehead by a Larry Doby line drive. The groan was when he fell on the pitcher's mound like a tagged prizefighter. And the cheer was when he picked himself up and gestured that he was okay. Which he

64

was not, but he pitched the rest of the sixth, and the seventh, too. Didn't give up a run, either. Ganzie made him come out before the eighth when he saw The Doo wasn't walking straight. Danny all the time claiming he was perfectly okay, that the big purple goose-egg raising up over his left eyebrow wasn't nothing, he'd had lots worse, and the kid saying the same: It ain't nothing, it ain't nothing. Little Sir Echo. Us down in the clubhouse didn't know any of that, no more than Dusen knew he might've been tagged worse in his career, but it was the first time part of his brain had sprung a leak.

"His name isn't Blakely," Lombardazzi says. "It's Eugene Katsanis."

"Katz-*whatsis*? Where's Blakely, then?"

"William Blakely's dead. Has been for a month. His parents, too."

I gaped at him. "What are you talking about?"

So he told me the stuff I'm sure you already know, Mr. King, but maybe I can fill in a few blanks. The Blakelys lived in Clarence, Iowa, a wide patch of not much an hour's drive from Davenport. Made it convenient for Ma and Pa, because they could go to most of their son's Minor League games. Blakely had a successful farm; an eight hundred acre job. One of their hired men wasn't much more than a boy. His name was Gene Katsanis, an orphan who'd grown up in The Ottershaw Christian Home for Boys. He was no farmer, and not quite right in the head, but he was a hell of a baseball player.

Katsanis and Blakely played against each other on a couple of church teams, and together on the local Babe Ruth team, which won the state tournament all three years the two of them played together, and once went as far as the national semis. Blakely went to high school and starred on that team, too, but Katsanis wasn't school material. Slopping-the-hogs material and ballplaying material is what he was, although he was never supposed to be as good as Billy Blakely. Nobody so much as considered such a thing. Until it happened, that is.

Blakely's father hired him because the kid worked cheap, sure, but mostly because he had enough natural talent to keep Billy sharp. For twenty-five dollars a week, the kid got a fielder and a batting-practice pitcher. The old man got a cow-milker and a shit-shoveler. Not a bad deal, at least for them.

Whatever you've found in your research probably favors the Blakely family, am I right? Because they had been around those parts for four generations, because they were rich farmers, and because Katsanis wasn't nothing but a state kid who started life in a liquor carton on a church step and had several screws loose upstairs. And why was that? Because he was born dumb or because he got the crap beaten out of him three and four times a week in that home before he got old enough and big enough to defend himself? I know a lot of the beatings came because he had a habit of talking to himself—that came out in the newspapers later on.

Katsanis and Billy practiced just as hard once Billy got into the Titans' farm system—during the off-season, you know, probably throwing and hitting in the barn once the snow got too deep outside—but Katsanis got kicked off the local town team, and wasn't allowed to go to the Cornholers' workouts during Billy's second season with them. During his first one, Katsanis had been allowed to participate in some of the workouts, even in some intersquad games, if they were a man shy. It was all pretty informal and loosey-goosey back then, not like now when the insurance companies shit a brick if a Major Leaguer so much as grabs a bat without wearing a helmet.

What I think happened—feel free to correct me if you know better—is that the kid, whatever other problems he might have had, continued to grow and mature as a ballplayer. Blakely didn't. You see that all the time. Two kids who both look like Babe Fuckin' Ruth in high school. Same height, same weight, same speed, same twenty-twenty peepers. But one of them is able to play at the next level . . . and the next . . . and the next . . . while the other one starts to fall behind. This much I did hear later: Billy Blakely didn't start out as a catcher. He got switched from center field when the kid who *was* catching broke his arm. And that kind of switch isn't a real good sign. It's like the coach is sending a message: "You'll do . . . but only until someone better shows up."

Blockade Billy

I think Blakely got jealous, I think his old man got jealous, and I think maybe Mom did, too. Maybe especially Mom, because sports moms can be the worst. I think maybe they pulled a few strings to keep Katsanis from playing locally, and from showing up for the Davenport Cocksuckers' workouts. They could have done it, because they were a wealthy, long-established Iowa family and Gene Katsanis was a nobody who grew up in an orphan home. A *Christian* orphan home that was probably hell on earth.

I think maybe Billy got ragging on the kid once too often and once too hard. Or it could've been the dad or the mom. Maybe it was over the way he milked the cows, or maybe he didn't shovel the shit just right that one time, but I'll bet the bottom line was baseball and plain old jealousy. The green-eyed monster. For all I know, the Cornholers' manager told Blakely he might be sent down to Single A in Clearwater, and getting sent down a rung when you're only twenty—when you're supposed to be going *up* the ladder—is a damned good sign that your career in organized baseball is going to be a short one.

But however it was—and *whoever*—it was a bad mistake. The kid could be sweet when he was treated right, we all knew that, but he wasn't right in the head. And he could be dangerous. I knew that even before the cops showed up, because of what happened in the very first game of the season: Billy Anderson.

"The County Sheriff found all three Blakelys in the barn," Lombardazzi said. "Katsanis slashed their throats. Sheriff said it looked like a razor blade."

I just gaped at him.

"What must have happened is this," Joe said in a heavy voice. "Kerwin McCaslin called around for a backup catcher when our guys got hurt down in Florida, and the manager of the Cornhuskers said he had a boy who might fill the bill for three or four weeks, assuming we didn't need him to hit for average. Because, he said, this kid wouldn't do that."

"But he did," I says.

"Because he wasn't Blakely," Lombardazzi says. "By then Blakely and his parents must already have been dead a couple of days, at least. The Katsanis kid was keeping house all by himself. And not *all* his screws were loose. He was smart enough to answer the phone when it rang. He took the call from the manager and said sure, Billy'd be glad to go to New Jersey. And before he left—as Billy—he called around to the neighbors and the feed store downtown. Told em the Blakelys had been called away on a family emergency and he was taking care of things. Pretty smart for a loony, wouldn't you say?"

"He's not a loony," I told him.

"Well, he cut the throats of the people who took him in and gave him a job, and he killed all the cows so the neighbors wouldn't hear them bawling to be milked at night, but have it your way. I know the DA's going to agree with you, because he wants to see Katsanis get the rope. That's how they do it in Iowa, you know."

I turned to Joe. "How could a thing like this happen?"

"Because he was good," Joe said. "And because he wanted to play ball."

The kid had Billy Blakely's ID, and this was back in the days when picture IDs were pretty much unheard of. The two kids matched up pretty well: blue eyes, dark hair, six feet tall. But mostly, yeah—it happened because the kid was good. And wanted to play ball.

"Good enough to get almost a month in the pros," Lombardazzi said, and over our heads a cheer went up. Billy Blockade had just gotten his last big-league hit: a homer. "Then, day before yesterday, the LP gas man went out to the Blakely farm. Other folks had been there before, but they read the note Katsanis left on the door and went away. Not the gas man. He filled the tanks behind the barn, and the barn was where the bodies were—cows and Blakelys both. The weather had finally turned warm, and he smelled em. Which is pretty much the way our story ends. Now, your manager here wants him arrested with as little fuss as possible, and with as little danger to the other players on your team as possible. That's fine with me. So your job—"

"Your job is to hold the rest of the guys in the dugout," Jersey Joe says. "Send Blakely . . . Katsanis . . . down here on his own. He'll be gone when the rest of the guys get to the locker room. Then we'll try to sort this clusterfuck out."

"What the hell do I tell them?"

"Team meeting. Free ice cream. I don't care. You just hold them for five minutes."

I says to Lombardazzi, "No one tipped? *No one?* You mean no one heard the radio broadcasts and tried calling Pop Blakely to say how great it was that his kid was tearing up the bigs?"

"I imagine one or two might have tried," Lombardazzi said. "Folks from Iowa *do* come to the big city from time to time, I'm told, and I imagine a few people visiting New York listen to the Titans or read about em in the paper—"

"I prefer the Yankees," one of the bluesuits chimes in.

"If I want your opinion, I'll rattle the bars in your cage," Lombardazzi said. "Until then, shut up and die right."

I looked at Joe, feeling sick. Getting a bad call and getting run off the field during my first managerial stint now seemed like the very least of my problems.

"Get him in here alone," Joe said. "I don't care how. The guys shouldn't have to see this." He thought it over and added: "And the kid shouldn't have to *see* them seeing it. No matter what he did."

If it matters—and I know it don't—we lost that game two to one. All three runs were solo shots. Minnie Minoso hit the game-winner off of Ganzie in the top of the ninth. The kid made the final out. He whiffed in his first at-bat as a Titan; he whiffed in his last one. Baseball is also a game of balance.

But none of our guys cared about the game. When I got up there, they were gathered around The Doo, who was sitting on the bench and telling them he was fine, goddammit, just a little dizzy. But he didn't look fine, and our old excuse for a doc looked pretty grave. He wanted Danny down at Newark General for X-rays.

"Fuck that," Doo says. "I just need a couple of minutes. I'm all right, I tell you. Jesus, Bones, cut me a break."

"Blakely," I said. "Go on down to the locker room. Mr. DiPunno wants to see you."

"Coach DiPunno wants to see me? In the locker room? Why?"

"Something about the Rookie of the Month award,"

I said. It just popped into my head from nowhere. There was no such thing back then, but the kid didn't know that.

The kid looks at Danny Doo, and The Doo flaps his hand at him. "Go on, get out of here, kid. You played a good game. Not your fault. You're still lucky, and fuck anyone who says different." Then he says: "All of you get out of here. Gimme some breathing-room."

"Hold off on that," I says. "Joe wants to see him alone. Give him a little one-to-one congratulations, I guess. Kid, don't wait around. Just—" *Just scat* was how I meant to finish, but I didn't have to. Blakely or Katsanis, he was already gone. And you know what happened after that.

If the kid had gone straight down the hall to the umpire's room, he would have gotten collared, because the locker room was on the way. Instead, he cut through our box-room, where luggage was stored and where we also had a couple of massage tables and a whirlpool bath. We'll never know for sure why he did that, but I think the kid knew something was wrong. Crazy or not, he must have known the roof was going to fall in on him eventually. In any case, he came out on the far side of the locker room, walked down to the ump's room, and knocked on the door. By then the rig he probably learned how to make in The Ottershaw Christian Home was back on his second finger. One of the older boys probably showed him how, that's what I think. *Kid, if you want to stop getting beaten up all the time, make yourself one of these.*

He never put it back in his locker after all, you see; just tucked it into his pocket. And he didn't bother with the Band-Aid after the game, which tells me he knew he didn't have anything to hide anymore.

He raps on the umpire's door and says, "Urgent telegram for Mr. Hi Wenders." Crazy but not stupid, you see? I don't know what would have happened if one of the other umps on the crew had opened up, but it was Wenders himself, and I'm betting his life was over even before he realized it wasn't a Western Union delivery-boy standing there.

It *was* a razor blade, see? Or a piece of one, anyway. When it wasn't needed, it stayed inside a little tin band like a kid's pretend finger-ring. Only when he balled

his right fist and pushed on the band with the ball of
his thumb, that little sliver of a blade popped up on a
spring. Wenders opened the door and Katsanis swept
it across his neck and cut his throat with it. When I
saw the puddle of blood after he was taken away in
handcuffs—oh my God, such a pool of it there was—
all I could think of was those forty thousand people
screaming *KILL THE UMP* the same way they'd been
screaming *Bloh-KADE*. No one really means it, but
the kid didn't know that, either. Especially not after
The Doo poured a lot of poison in his ears about how
Wenders was out to get *both* of them.

When the cops ran out of the locker room, Billy
Blockade was just standing there with blood all down
the front of his white home uniform and Wenders lying
at his feet. Nor did he try to fight or slash when the blue-
suits grabbed him. No, he just stood there whispering
to himself. "I got him, Doo. I got him, Billy. He won't
make no more bad calls now. I got him for all of us."

That's where the story ends, Mr. King—the part of
it I know, at least. As far as the Titans go, you could
look it up, as ol' Casey used to say: All those games

canceled out, and all the doubleheaders we played to make them up. How we ended up with old Hubie Rattner behind the plate after all, and how he batted .185—well below what they now call the Mendoza Line. How Danny Dusen was diagnosed with something called "an intercranial bleed" and had to sit out the rest of the season. How he tried to come back in 1958—that was sad. Five outings. In three of them he couldn't get the ball over the plate. In the other two . . . do you remember the last Red Sox–Yankees playoff game in 2004? How Kevin Brown started for the Yankees, and the Sox scored six goddam runs off him in the first two innings? That's how Danny Doo pitched in '58 when he actually managed to get the ball over the dish. He had *nothing*. And still, after all that, we managed to finish ahead of the Senators and the Athletics. Only Jersey Joe DiPunno had a heart attack during the World Series that year. Might have been the same day the Russians put the Sputnik up. They took him out of County Stadium on a stretcher. He lived another five years, but he was a shadow of his former self and of course he never managed again.

He said the kid sucked luck, and he was more right than he knew. Mr. King, that kid was a *black hole* for luck.

For himself, as well. I'm sure you know how his story ended—how he was taken to Essex County Jail and held there for extradition. How he swallowed a bar of soap and choked to death on it. I can't think of a worse way to go. That was a nightmare season, no doubt, and still, telling you about it brought back some good memories. Mostly, I think, of how Old Swampy would flush orange when all those fans raised their signs: ROAD CLOSED BY ORDER OF BLOCK-ADE BILLY. Yep, I bet the fellow who thought those up made a goddam mint. But you know, the people who bought them got fair value. When they stood up with them held over their heads, they were part of something bigger than themselves. That can be a bad thing—just think of all the people who turned out to see Hitler at his rallies—but this was a good thing. *Baseball* is a good thing. Always was, always will be.

Bloh-KADE, bloh-KADE, bloh-KADE.

Still gives me a chill to think of it. Still echoes in

my head. That kid was the real thing, crazy or not, luck-sucker or not.

Mr. King, I think I'm all talked out. Do you have enough? Good. I'm glad. You come back anytime you want, but not on Wednesday afternoon; that's when they have their goddam Virtual Bowling, and you can't hear yourself think. Come on Saturday, why don't you? There's a bunch of us always watches the Game of the Week. We're allowed a couple of beers, and we root like mad bastards. It ain't like the old days, but it ain't bad.

MORALITY

1 .

Chad knew something was up as soon as he walked in. Nora was home already. Her hours were from eleven to five, six days a week; the way it usually worked, he got home from school at four and had dinner on when she came in around six.

She was sitting on the fire escape, where he went to smoke, and she had some paperwork in her hands. He looked at the refrigerator and saw that the e-mail printout was gone from beneath the magnet that had been holding it in place for almost four months.

"Hey, you," she said. "Come on out here." She paused. "Bring your butts, if you want."

He was down to just a pack a week, but that didn't make her like his habit any better. The health issue was part of it, but the expense was an even bigger part. Every cigarette was forty cents up in smoke.

He climbed out and sat down beside her. She had changed into jeans and one of her old blouses, so she had been home for a while. Stranger and stranger.

They looked out over their little bit of the city for a while without speaking. He kissed her and she smiled in an absent way. She had the agent's e-mail; she also had the file folder with THE RED AND THE BLACK written on it in big capitals. His little joke, but not so funny. The file contained their financial stuff—bank and credit-card statements, utility bills, insurance premiums—and the bottom line was all red. It was an American story these days: just not enough. Two years ago they'd talked about having a kid. What they talked about now was getting out from under and maybe enough ahead to leave the city without a bunch of creditors snapping at their heels. Move north to New England. But not yet. At least here they were working.

"How was school?" she asked.

"Fine."

Actually, the job was a plum. But after Anita Biderman got back from maternity leave, who knew? Probably not another job at P.S. 321. He was high on the list of subs, but that didn't mean anything if the regular teaching roster was all present and accounted for. Sometimes, lying in bed and waiting for sleep to overtake him, he thought of the little boy in the D. H. Lawrence story who rode his rocking horse crying, "There *must* be more money!"

"You're home early," he said. "Don't tell me Winnie died."

She looked startled, then smiled. But they had been together for ten years, married for the last six, and Chad knew when something was wrong.

"Nora?"

"He sent me home early. To think. I've got a lot to think about. I'm . . ." She shook her head.

He took her by the shoulder and turned her to him. "You're what, Norrie? Is everything okay?"

"Go on, light up. Smoking lamp's lit."

"Tell me what's going on."

She had been cut from the staff of Congress Memorial Hospital two years ago during a "reorganization." Luckily for the Chad-and-Nora Corporation, she had landed on her feet. Getting the home-nursing job had been a coup: one patient, a retired minister recovering from a stroke, thirty-six hours a week, very decent wages. She made more than he did, and by a good bit. The two incomes were almost enough to live on. At least until Anita Biderman came back.

"First, let's talk about this." She held up the agent's e-mail. "How sure are you?"

"That I can do the work? Pretty sure. Almost positive. I mean, if I had the time. About the rest . . ." He shrugged. "It's right there in black and white—no guarantees."

With the hiring freeze currently in effect in the city's schools, subbing was the best Chad could do. He was on every list in the system, but there was no full-time position in his immediate future. Nor would the money be much better even if such a position opened up—just more reliable. As a sub, he sometimes spent weeks on the bench.

Out of desperation and a need to fill up the empty hours when Nora was tending to the Reverend Winston, Chad had started a book he called *Living with the Animals: The Life of a Substitute Teacher in Four City Schools*. Words did not come easily to him, and on some days they did not come at all, but by the time he was called in to St. Saviour to teach second grade (Mr. Cardelli had broken a leg in a car accident), he had finished three chapters. Nora received the pages with a troubled smile. No woman wants the job of telling the man in her life that he's been wasting his time.

He hadn't been. The stories he told of the substitute teaching life were sweet, funny, and often moving— much more interesting than anything she'd heard over dinner or while they were lying in bed together.

He finally found an agent who would at least look at the eighty pages he had managed to wring out of his old and limping Dell laptop. The agent's name had a circusy feel: Edward Ringling. His response to Chad's pages was long on praise and short on promise. "I might be able to get you a book contract based on this and an outline of the rest," Ringling had written, "but it would be a very small contract, likely a good deal less than you currently make as a teacher. What I suggest is that you finish another seven or eight chapters, possibly even the whole book. Then I might be able to take it to auction and get you a much better deal."

It made sense, Chad supposed, if you were oversee-ing the literary world from a comfy office in Manhat-tan. Not so much if you were hopscotching all over the boroughs, teaching a week here and three days there, trying to keep ahead of the bills. Ringling's letter had come in May. Now it was September, and although Chad had had a relatively good few months teaching summer school (*God bless the dummies,* he sometimes thought), he hadn't added a single page to the manu-script. It wasn't laziness; teaching, even when it was just subbing, was like having a pair of jumper cables attached to some critical part of your brain.

"How long would it take to finish it?" Nora asked. "If you were writing full-time?"

He drew out his cigarettes and lit one. He felt a strong urge to give an overoptimistic answer but over-came it. Whatever was going on with her, she deserved the truth.

"Eight months at least."

"And how much money do you think it would mean if Mr. Ringling held an auction?"

On this Chad had done his homework. "I'd guess the advance could be in the neighborhood of $100,000."

A fresh start in Vermont, that was the plan. That was what they talked about in bed. A small town, maybe up in the Northeast Kingdom. She could catch on at the local hospital or get another private; he could land a full-time teaching position. Or just maybe write another book.

"Nora, what's this about?"

"I'm afraid to tell you, but I will. Crazy or not, I will. Because the number Winnie mentioned was bigger than $100,000. Only one thing: I'm not quitting my job. He said I could keep it no matter what we decided, and we *need* that job."

He reached for the aluminum ashtray he kept tucked under the windowsill and butted his cigarette in it. Then he took her hand. "Tell me."

He listened with amazement but not disbelief. He sort of wished he could disbelieve it, but he did not.

What had she actually known about Reverend George Winston? That he was a lifelong bachelor, that three years into his retirement from the Second Presbyterian Church of Park Slope (where he was still listed on the church slate as Pastor Emeritus), he had suffered a stroke. That the stroke had left him partially paralyzed on the right side and in need of home care. Not much more.

He could now walk to the bathroom (and, on good days, to his front-porch rocker) with the help of a plastic brace that kept his bad knee from buckling. And he could talk understandably again, although he still sometimes suffered from what Nora called "sleepy tongue." Nora had previous experience with stroke victims (it was what had clinched the job), and she had a great appreciation for how far he had come in a short time.

In addition to such nursely duties as giving him his pills and monitoring his blood pressure, she worked with him as a physical therapist. She was also a masseuse and occasionally—when he had letters to write—a secretary. She ran errands and sometimes read to him. And she wasn't above light housekeeping on days when Mrs. Granger did not come in. On those days she made sandwiches or omelets for lunch, and she supposed it was over those lunches that he had drawn out the details of her own life—and had done it without Nora ever realizing what was going on.

"The one thing I remember saying," she told Chad, "and probably only because he mentioned it today, was that we weren't living in abject poverty or even in discomfort. It was the *fear* of those things that got us down."

Chad smiled at that.

This morning Winnie had refused both the sponge bath and the massage. Instead, he had asked her to put on his brace and help him into his study, which was a relatively long walk for him, certainly farther than the porch rocker. He made it and fell into the chair behind his desk, red-faced and panting. He drained the glass of orange juice she gave him in a single go.

"Thank you, Nora. I want to talk to you now. Very seriously."

He must have seen her apprehension, because he smiled and made a waving-off gesture. "It's not about your job. You'll have that no matter what. If you want it. If not, I'll see that you have a reference that can't be beat."

"You're making me nervous, Winnie," she said.

"How would you like to make $200,000?"

She gawked. All around them, high shelves of smart

books frowned down. The noises from the street were muffled. They might have been in another country. A quieter country than Brooklyn.

"If you think this is about sex—it occurred to me that you might—I assure you it is not. At least I don't think so; if one looks below the surface, and if one has read Freud, I suppose any aberrant act may be said to have a sexual basis. I don't know myself. I haven't studied Freud since seminary, and even then my reading was cursory. Freud offended me. He seemed to feel that any suggestion of depth in human nature was an illusion. He seemed to be saying, What you think is a pool is a puddle. I beg to differ. Human nature has no bottom. It is as deep and mysterious as the mind of God."

"With all respect, I'm not sure I believe in God. And I'm not sure this is a proposal I want to hear."

"But if you don't listen, you won't know. And you'll always wonder."

She was unsure what to do or say. What she thought was, *That desk he's sitting behind must have cost thousands*. It was the first time she had really thought of him in connection with money.

"What I'm offering should be enough to pay off all

your outstanding bills, enough to enable your husband to finish his book—enough, perhaps, to start a new life in . . . was it Vermont?"

"Yes."

"Cash, Nora. No need to get the IRS involved." He had long features and white woolly hair. A sheeplike face, she had always thought before today. "Cash causes no problems if it's fed slowly into the stream of one's accounts. Also, once your husband's book is sold and you're established in New England, we need never see each other again." He paused. "Although we could. That part would be up to you. And please relax. You're sitting bolt upright."

It was the thought of $200,000 that kept her in the room. Two hundred thousand in cash. She found she could actually see it: bills stuffed into a padded manila envelope. Or perhaps it would take two envelopes to hold that much.

"Let me talk for a bit," he said. "I haven't really done much of that, have I? Mostly I've listened. It's your turn to listen now, Nora. Will you do that?"

"I suppose." She was very curious. She supposed anybody would be. "Who do you want me to kill?"

It was a joke, but as soon as it was out of her mouth, she was afraid it might be true. Because it didn't *sound* like a joke. No more than the eyes in his long sheep's face looked like sheep's eyes.

Winnie laughed. Then he said, "Not murder, my dear. We won't need to go that far."

He talked then as he never had before. To anyone, probably.

"I grew up wealthy on Long Island—my father was successful in the market. He survived my mother by only five years, and when he passed on, I inherited a great deal of money, mostly in bonds and solid stocks. Over the years since, I have converted a small percentage of that to cash, a bit at a time. Not a nest egg, because I've never needed one, but what I'd call a *wish* egg. It's in a Manhattan safe-deposit box, and it's that cash that I'm offering you, Nora. It may actually be closer to $240,000, but we'll agree, shall we, not to quibble over a dollar here and a dollar there?

"My life has been one—I say it with neither pride

nor shame—of unremarkable service. I have led my church in helping the poor, both in countries far from here and in this community. The AA drop-in center up the street was my idea, and it's helped hundreds of suffering alcoholics and addicts. I've comforted the sick and buried the dead. More cheerfully, I've presided over more than a thousand weddings, and inaugurated a scholarship fund that has sent many boys and girls to colleges they could not otherwise have afforded.

"I have only one regret: In all my years, I've never committed one of the sins I've spent a lifetime warning my various flocks about. I am not a lustful man, and since I've never been married, I've never had the opportunity to commit adultery. I'm not gluttonous by nature, and although I like nice things, I've never been greedy or covetous. Why would I be, when my father left me $15 million? I've worked hard, keep my temper, envy no one—except perhaps Mother Teresa—and have little pride of possessions or position.

"I'm not claiming I'm *without* sin. Not at all. Those who can say (and I suppose there are a few) that they have never sinned in deed or word can hardly say they've never sinned in thought, can they? The church covers every loophole. We hold out heaven, then make people understand they have no hope of achieving it without our help. . . . Because no one is without sin, and the wages of sin is death.

"I suppose this makes me sound like an unbeliever, but raised as I was, unbelief is as impossible for me as levitation. Yet I understand the cozening nature of the bargain, and the psychological tricks believers use to ensure the prosperity of those beliefs. The pope's fancy hat was not conferred on him by God but by men and women paying theological blackmail money.

"I can see you fidgeting, so I'll come to the point. I want to commit a major sin before I die. A sin not of thought or word but of deed. This was on my mind—increasingly on my mind—before my stroke, but I thought it a frenzy that would pass. Now I see that it will not, because the idea has been with me more than ever during the last three years. But how great a sin can an old man stuck in a wheelchair commit, I asked myself? Then, listening to you talk about your husband's book and your financial situation, it occurred to me that I could sin by proxy. In fact, I could double my sin quotient, as it were, by making you my accessory."

She spoke from a dry mouth. "I believe in wrongdoing, Winnie, but I don't believe in sin."

He smiled. It was a benevolent smile. Also unpleasant: sheep's lips, wolf's teeth. "That's fine. But sin believes in you. And . . . do you know what doubles sin?"

"No. I don't go to church."

"What doubles it is saying to yourself, *I will do this because I know I can pray for forgiveness once it's done.* To say to yourself that you can have your cake and eat it, too. I want to know what being that deep in sin is like. I don't want to wallow—I want to dive in over my head."

"And take me with you!" she said with real indignation.

"But you don't believe in sin, Nora, you just said so. From your standpoint, all I want is for you to get a little dirty. And risk arrest, I suppose, although the risk should be minor. For these things, I will pay you $200,000."

Her face and hands felt as if she had just come in

from a long walk in the cold. She would not do it, of course. What she would do was walk out of this house and get some fresh air. She wouldn't quit, or at least not immediately, because she needed the job, but she *would* walk out. And if he fired her for deserting her post, let him. But first, she wanted to hear the rest.

"What is it you want me to do?"

Chad had lit another cigarette. "What was it?"

She motioned with her fingers. "Give me a drag on that."

"Norrie, you haven't smoked a cigarette in five—"

"Give me a drag, I said."

He passed the cigarette to her. She dragged deep, coughed the smoke out, then told him the rest.

She lay awake late into the night, sure he was sleeping, and why not? The decision had been made. She would tell Winnie no and never mention the idea again. Decision made; sleep follows.

Still, she wasn't entirely surprised when he turned to her and said, "I can't stop thinking about it."

Nor could she. "I'd do it, you know. For us. If . . ."

Now they were face-to-face, inches apart. Close enough to taste each other's breath. It was two o'clock in the morning: the hour of conspiracy if there ever was one, she thought.

"If what?"

"If I didn't think it would taint our lives. Some stains don't come out."

"It's a moot question, Nor. We've decided. You play Sarah Palin and tell him thanks but no thanks for that bridge to nowhere. I'll find a way to finish the book without his psycho idea of a grant-in-aid."

"When? On your next unpaid leave? I don't think so."

"It's decided. He's nuts. The end." He rolled away from her.

Silence descended. Upstairs, Mrs. Reston—whose picture belonged in the dictionary next to *insomnia*—walked back and forth. Somewhere, maybe in deepest, darkest Gowanus, a siren wailed.

Fifteen minutes went by before Chad spoke to the end table and the digital clock, which now read 2:17A.

"Also, we'd have to trust him for the money, and you can't trust a man whose one remaining ambition in life is to commit a sin."

"But I *do* trust him," she said. "It's myself I don't trust. Go to sleep, Chad. This subject is closed."

"Right back atcha," he said.

The clock read 2:26A when she said, "It *could* be done. I'm sure of that much. I could change my hair color. Wear a hat. Dark glasses, of course. And there would have to be an escape route."

"Are you seriously—"

"I don't know. I'd have to work almost three years to make $200,000, and after the government and the banks wet their beaks, there'd be next to nothing left. We know how that works."

She was quiet for a minute, looking at the ceiling above which Mrs. Reston trudged her slow miles.

"And what if you got hit by a car? Or I turned up with an ovarian cyst?"

"Our coverage is okay."

"That's what everyone says, but what everyone knows is they fuck you at the drive-through. With this, we could be sure. That's what I keep thinking about. *Sure!*"

"Two hundred thousand dollars makes my financial hopes for the book seem kind of small, though, don't you think? Why even bother?"

"Because this would be a onetime thing. And the book would be clean."

"*Clean?* You think this would make the book *clean?*" He rolled over and faced her. Part of him had grown hard, so perhaps part of this *was* about sex. Who knew about such things? Who wanted to?

"Do you think I'll ever get another job like the one with Winnie?"

He said nothing to this, which was an answer in itself.

"And I'm not getting any younger. I'll be thirty-six in December. You'll take me to dinner for my birthday and a week later I'll get my real present: a past-due notice for the car-loan payment."

"Are you blaming me for—"

"*No.* I'm not even blaming the system. Blame is counterproductive. And I told Winnie the truth: I don't believe in sin. But I also don't want to go to jail." She felt tears growing in her eyes. "I don't want to hurt anyone, either. Especially not a—"

"You're not going to."

He started to turn over, but she grabbed his shoulder.

"If we did it—if *I* did it—we could never talk about it afterward. Not one single time."

"No."

She reached for him. In marriages, deals were sealed with more than a handshake. This they both knew.

The clock said 2:58A. Outside and below, a street sweeper went hushing by. He was drifting to sleep when she said, "Do you know anyone with a video camera? Because he wants—"

"Charlie Green has one."

After that, silence. Except for Mrs. Reston, still walking slowly back and forth above them. Mrs. Reston patiently walking off all those night miles. Then Nora fell asleep.

Her mother had never been a churchgoer, but Nora had attended Vacation Bible School every summer and enjoyed it. There were games and songs and flannel-board stories. She found herself remembering one of the stories the next day, in Winnie's study.

"I wouldn't have to really hurt the . . . you know, the person . . . to get the money?" she asked him. "I want to be very clear about that."

"No, but I expect to see blood flow. Let *me* be clear about *that*. I want you to use your fist, but a cut lip or bloody nose will be quite sufficient."

For the story, the teacher put a mountain on the flannel board. Then Jesus. Then the devil. The teacher said the devil had taken Jesus up on the mountain and showed him all the cities of the earth. *You can have everything in those cities,* the devil said. *Every treasure. All you have to do is fall down and worship me.* But Jesus was a stand-up guy. Jesus had said thanks but no thanks.

"Sin," she mused. "That's what's on your mind."

"Sin for its own sake. Deliberately planned and executed. Do you find the idea exciting?"

"No," she said, looking up at the frowning book-shelves.

Winnie let some time pass, then said, "Well?"

"If I got caught, would I still get the money?"

"If you lived up to your part of the agreement—and didn't implicate me, of course—you certainly would. And even if you were caught, the very worst to come of it would be probation."

"Plus court-ordered psychiatric evaluation," she said. "Which I probably need for even considering this."

Winnie said, "If you continue the way you are, dear, you'll need a marriage counselor, at the very least. In my time in the ministry, I counseled many partners, and while money worries weren't always the root cause of their problems, that's what it was in most cases. And that's *all* it was."

"Thank you for the benefit of your experience, Winnie."

He said nothing to this.

"You're crazy, you know."

He still said nothing.

She looked at the books some more. Most of them were on religion. Finally she turned her eyes back to his. "If I do this and you fuck me, I'll make you sorry."

He showed no discomfiture at her choice of language. "I'll honor my commitment. You may be sure of that."

"You speak almost perfectly now. Not even a lisp, unless you're tired."

He shrugged. "Being with me has trained your ear. It's like learning to understand a new language, I suppose."

She returned her eyes to the books. One of them was called *The Problem of Good and Evil.* Another was titled *The Basis of Morality.* It was a thick one. In the hall, an old regulator clock was ticking steadily. Finally he said it again: "Well?"

The regulator ticked. Without looking at him, she said, "If you say 'well' again, I'll walk out of here."

He didn't say "well" or anything else. She looked down at her hands, twisting in her lap. The most appalling thing: Part of her was still curious. Not about what he wanted, that cat was out of the bag, but about what she wanted.

At last she looked up and gave her answer.

"Excellent," he said.

With the decision made, neither Chad nor Nora wanted the actual act hanging over their heads; it cast too big a shadow. They chose Forest Park in Queens. Chad borrowed Charlie Green's video camera and learned how to use it. They went to the park twice beforehand (on rainy days when it was mostly empty), and Chad videotaped the area they decided on. They had a lot of sex during that period—nervous sex, fumbling sex, but usually good sex. Hot, at least. Nora found her other major appetites dwindling. In the ten days between her agreement and the morning when she executed her part of the bargain, she lost nine pounds. Chad said she was starting to look like a teenager again.

On a sunny day in early October, Chad parked their old Ford on Myrtle Avenue. Nora sat beside him, her hair dyed red and hanging to her shoulders, looking very un-Nora-like in a long skirt and an ugly brown smock top. She was wearing sunglasses and a Mets cap. She seemed calm enough, but when he reached out to touch her, she twitched away.

"Nor, c'mon—"

"Have you got cab fare?"

"Yes."

"And a bag to put the videocam in?"

"Yes, of course."

"Then give me the car keys. I'll see you back at the apartment."

"Are you sure you'll be able to drive? Because the reaction to something like this—"

"I'll be fine. Give me the keys. Wait here fifteen minutes. If there's something wrong . . . if anything even *feels* wrong, I'll come back. If I don't, you go to the spot we picked out. Do you remember it?"

"Of course I remember it!"

She smiled—showed her teeth and dimples at least. "That's the spirit," she said, and was gone.

It was an excruciatingly long fifteen minutes, but Chad waited through every one of them. Kids wearing clamshell helmets pooted past on bikes. Women strolled in pairs, many with shopping bags. He saw an old lady laboriously crossing the avenue, and for a moment he thought it was Mrs. Reston, but when she passed by, he saw that it wasn't. This woman was much older than Mrs. Reston.

When the fifteen minutes were almost up, it occurred to him—in a sane and rational way—that he could put a stop to this by driving away. The extra ignition key was hidden beneath the spare tire. In the park, Nora would look around and not see him. She would be the one to take the cab back to Brooklyn. And when she got there, she would thank him. She would say, *You saved me from myself.*

After that? Take a month off. No substitute teaching. He would turn all his resources to finishing the book. Throw his cap over the windmill.

Instead, he got out and walked to the park with Charlie Green's video camera in his hand. The paper bag that would hold it afterward was stuffed in the pocket of his windbreaker. He checked three times to make sure the camera's green power light was glowing. How terrible it would be to go through all this and discover he'd never turned on the camera. Or that he'd left the lens cap on.

Nora was sitting on a park bench. When she saw him, she brushed her hair back from the left side of her face. That was the signal: It was on.

Behind her was a playground—swings, a push merry-go-round, teeter-totters, bouncy horses on springs, that sort of thing. At this hour, there were only a few kids playing. The moms were in a group on the far side, talking and laughing, not really paying much attention to the kids.

Nora got up from the bench.

Two hundred thousand dollars, he thought, and raised the camera to his eye. Now that it was on, he felt calm.

2.

Back at their building, Chad raced up the stairs. He felt sure that she wouldn't be there. He had seen her go skimming away at a full-out run, and the mothers had barely given her a look—they were converging on the child she had chosen, a boy of perhaps four—but he was still sure she wouldn't be there and that he would get a call telling him that his wife was at the police station, where she had collapsed and told everything, including his part in it. Worse, Winnie's part in it, thus ensuring it had all been for nothing.

His hand was shaking so badly that he couldn't get the key into the slot; it went chattering madly around the key plate without even coming close. He was in the act of putting down the paper bag (now badly crumpled) with the videocam inside it so he could use his left hand to steady his right when the door opened.

Nora was now wearing cut-off jeans and a shell top, the clothes she'd had on beneath the long skirt and smock. The plan had been for her to change in the car, before driving away. She said she could do it like lightning, and it seemed she'd been right.

He threw his arms around her and hugged her so tightly, he heard the thump as she came against him— not exactly a romantic embrace.

Nora bore this for a moment, then said: "Get out of the hall." And as soon as the door to the outside world was closed, she said: "Did you get it? Tell me you did. I've been here for almost half an hour going nuts."

"I was worried, too." He shoved his hair off his forehead, where the skin felt hot and feverish. "Norrie, I was scared to *death*."

She snatched the bag from his hands, peered inside, then glared at him. She had ditched the sunglasses and her blue eyes burned. "*Tell me you got it.*"

"Yeah. That is, I think so. I *must* have. I haven't looked yet."

The glare got hotter. "You better have. You better have. The time I haven't been pacing around, I've been on the toilet. I keep having cramps—" She went to the window and looked out. He joined her, afraid she knew something he didn't. But there were only the usual pedestrians going back and forth.

She turned to him again and this time grabbed his arms. Her palms were dead cold. "Is he all right? The kid? Did you see if he was all right?"

"He's fine," Chad said.

"Are you lying?" She was shouting. "You better not be!"

"Fine, I said. Standing up even before the mothers got to him. Bawling his head off, but I got worse at that kid's age when I was clopped in the back of the head by a swing. I had to go to the emergency room and have five sti—"

"I hit him much harder than I meant to. I was so afraid that if I pulled the punch . . . if Winnie *saw* I pulled it . . . he wouldn't pay. And the *adrenaline* . . . Christ! It's a wonder I didn't tear that poor kid's head right off! Why did I ever do it?" But she wasn't crying, and she didn't look remorseful. She looked furious. "Why did you *let* me?"

"I never—"

"You really saw him getting up? Because I hit him much harder than I . . ." She wheeled away from him, went to the wall, knocked her forehead against it, then turned back. "I walked into a playground and I punched a four-year-old child square in the mouth! For *money*!"

He had an inspiration. "I think it's on the tape. The kid getting up, I mean. You'll see for yourself."

She flew back across the room. "Put it on! I want to see!"

Chad found the cable Charlie had given him. Then, after a little fumbling, he played the tape on the TV. He had indeed recorded the kid getting to his feet again just before shutting the thing off and walking away. The kid looked bewildered, and of course he was crying, but otherwise he seemed fine. His lips were bleeding quite a lot, but his nose only a little. Chad thought he might have gotten the bloody nose when he fell down.

No worse than any minor playground accident, he thought. *Thousands of them happen every day.*

"See?" he asked her. "He's fi—"

"Run it again."

He did. And when she asked him to run it a third time, and a fourth, and a fifth, he did that, too. At some point he became aware that she was no longer watching to see the kid get up. Neither was he. They were watching him go down. And the punch. The punch delivered by the crazy red-haired bitch in the sunglasses. The one who walked up and did her business and then took off with wings on her sneakers.

She said, "I think I knocked out one of his teeth."

He shrugged. "Good news for the Tooth Fairy."

After the fifth viewing, she said, "I want to get the red out of my hair. I hate it."

"Okay—"

"But first, take me in the bedroom. Don't talk about it, either. Just do it."

She kept telling him to go harder, almost belting him with her upthrusting hips, as if she wanted to buck him off. But she wasn't getting there.

"Hit me," she said.

He slapped her. He was beyond rationality.

"You can do better than that. Fucking *hit* me!"

He hit her harder. Her lower lip split open. She smeared her fingers through the blood. While she was doing it she came.

"Show it to me," Winnie said. This was the next day. They were in his study.

"Show me the money." A famous line. She just couldn't remember from where.

"After I see the video."

The camera was still in the crumpled bag. She took it out, along with the cable. He had a little TV in the study, and she connected the cable to it. She pushed play, and they looked at the woman in the Mets cap sitting on the park bench. Behind her, a few children were playing. Behind them, mommies were talking mommy shit: body wraps, plays they had seen or were going to see, the new car, the next vacation. Blah-blah-blah.

The woman got up from the bench. The camera zoomed jerkily in. The picture shivered a bit, then steadied.

Nora hit the pause button. This was Chad's idea, and she had agreed to it. She trusted Winnie, but only so far.

"The money."

Winnie took a key from the pocket of the cardigan sweater he was wearing. He used it to open the center drawer of his desk, switching it to his left hand when the partially paralyzed right one wouldn't do his bidding.

It wasn't an envelope after all. It was a medium-sized Federal Express box. She looked inside and saw bundled hundreds, each bundle secured with a rubber band.

He said, "It's all there, plus some extra."

"All right. Look at what you bought. All you have to do is push play. I'll be in the kitchen."

"Don't you want to watch it with me?"

"No."

"Nora? You appear to have had a small accident yourself." He tapped the corner of his mouth, the side that still turned down slightly.

Had she thought he had a sheep's face? How stupid of her. How unseeing. Nor was it a wolf's face, not really. It was somewhere in between. A dog's face maybe. The kind of dog that would bite and then run.

"I ran into a door," she said.

"I see."

"All right, I'll watch it with you," she said, and sat down. She pushed play herself.

They watched the video twice, in complete silence. The running time was about thirty seconds. That amounted to about $6,600 a second. Nora had done the math.

After the second time, he pushed stop. She showed him how to eject the small cassette. "This is yours. The camera has to go back to the guy my husband borrowed it from."

"I understand." His eyes were bright. "I shall have Mrs. Granger buy me another camera for future viewings. Or perhaps that's an errand you'd care to run."

"Not me. We're done."

"Ah." He didn't look surprised. "All right. But if I may make a suggestion . . . you may want to get another job. So no one thinks it odd your bills begin getting paid off at a faster clip. It's your welfare I'm thinking of, dear."

"I'm sure." She unplugged the cable and put it back in the bag with the camera.

"And I wouldn't leave for Vermont too soon."

"I don't need your advice. I feel dirty and you're the reason why."

"But you won't get caught and no one will ever know." The right side of his mouth was drawn down, the left side lifted in what could have been a smile. The result was a serpentine S below his beak of a nose. His speech was very clear that day. She would remember that and ponder it. As if what he called sin had turned out to be therapy. "And Nora . . . is feeling dirty always a bad thing?"

She had no idea how to answer this.

"I only ask," he said, "because the second time you ran the tape, I watched you instead of it."

She picked up the bag with Charlie Green's video-cam inside and walked to the door. "Have a nice life, Winnie. Make sure you get an actual therapist as well as a nurse next time. You can afford it. And take care of that tape. For both our sakes."

"You're unidentifiable on it, dear. And even if you weren't, would anyone care?" He shrugged. "It doesn't depict a rape or murder after all."

She stood in the doorway, wanting to be gone but curious. Still curious.

"Winnie, how will you square this with your God?"

He chuckled. "If a sinner like Simon Peter could go on to found the Catholic Church, I expect I'll be fine."

"Did Simon Peter keep the videotape to watch on cold winter evenings?"

This finally silenced him, and Nora left before he could find his voice again. It was a small victory, but one she grasped eagerly.

A week later he called the apartment and told her she was welcome to come back, at least until she and Chad left for Vermont.

"I miss you, Nora."

She said nothing.

His voice dropped. "We could watch the tape again. Wouldn't you like to do that? Wouldn't you like to see it again, at least once?"

"No," she said, and hung up. She started toward the kitchen to make tea, but then a wave of faintness came over her. She sat down in the corner of the living room and bent her head to her upraised knees. She waited for the faintness to pass. Eventually it did.

• • •

She got a job taking care of Mrs. Reston. It was only twenty hours a week, and the pay was nothing like what she had been making as Reverend Winston's employee, but money was no longer the issue, and the commute was easy: one flight of stairs. Best of all, Mrs. Reston, who suffered from diabetes and mild cardiac problems, was a featherbrained sweetie. Sometimes, however—especially during her endless monologues concerning her late husband—Nora's hand itched to reach out and slap her.

Chad kept his name on the sub list, but cut back on his hours. He set aside most of those newfound hours to work on *Living with the Animals.* The pages began to mount up.

Once or twice he asked himself if the new pages were as good—as lively—as the work he had done before that day with the video camera, and he told himself that the question had only occurred to him because some old and false notion of retribution was lodged in his mind. Like a kernel of popcorn between two back teeth.

• • •

Twelve days after the day in the park, there was a knock at the apartment door. When Nora opened it, a policeman was standing there.

"Yes?" she asked, and thought calmly: *I will confess everything. And after the authorities have done to me whatever they do, I'll go to that boy's mother and stick out my face and say, "Hit me with your best shot, Mama. You'll be doing us both a favor."*

He looked at his notebook. "If this is 3-C, that makes you Mrs. Callahan."

"Yes, I'm Mrs. Callahan."

"Ma'am, I'm here on a canvas. Because a mugger has been working the neighborhood. He hurt an elderly gentleman quite badly last night. Can I show you some pictures?"

"Of course, but I haven't seen——"

"I'm sure." He grinned to show her how silly it all was. She was thinking it was a very handsome grin. She was also thinking this could be a pretext. Getting a good look at the suspect. Sizing her up.

But when she had looked at eight pictures and recognized none of the men, he nodded and put them away. "Should I check back with your husband?"

"Up to you, but he wouldn't notice a two-headed man unless they bumped into each other on the street." She felt giddy with relief, but part of her continued to wonder if there was some other agenda at work here. *She* was a mugger, after all.

"I heard that. But if you see anyone in the neighborhood who looks like any of the pictures I showed you . . ."

"I'll call you first . . ." She looked at his name tag. "Officer Abromowitz."

He smiled. "You do that," he said.

That night, in bed.

"Hit me!" As though it were not lovemaking but some nightmare blackjack game.

"No."

She was on top, which made him easy to reach. The sound of her palm on the side of his face was like the report of an air gun.

Chad hit her back without thinking. She began

to cry. He did her. Outside, someone's car alarm went off.

They went to Vermont in January. They went on the train. It was lovely, like a picture postcard. They saw a house they both liked about twenty miles outside of Montpelier. It was only the third one they'd looked at.

The real estate agent's name was Jody Enders. She was very pleasant, but she kept looking at Nora's right eye. Finally Nora said, with an embarrassed little laugh, "I slipped on a patch of ice while I was getting into a taxi. You should have seen me last week. I looked like a spouse-abuse ad."

"I can hardly see it," Jody Enders said. Then, shyly: "You're very pretty."

Chad put his arm around Nora's shoulders. "I think so, too."

"What do you do for a living, Mr. Callahan?"

"I'm a writer," he said.

They made a down payment on the house. On the loan agreement, Nora checked OWNER FINANCED. In the DETAILS box, she wrote simply: *Savings*.

• • •

One day in February, while they were packing for the move, Chad went into Manhattan to see a movie at the Angelika and have dinner with his agent. Officer Abromowitz had given Nora his card. She called him. He came over and they fucked in the mostly empty bedroom. It was good, but it would have been better if she could have persuaded him to hit her. She asked, but he wouldn't.

"What kind of crazy lady are you?" he asked in that voice people use when they mean *I'm joking but not really.*

"I don't know," Nora said. "I'm still finding out. We live and learn, Officer Abromowitz. Don't we?"

They were scheduled to make the move to Vermont on February 29. The day before, the telephone rang. It was Mrs. Granger, Pastor Emeritus Winston's housekeeper. As soon as Nora registered the woman's hushed tone, she knew why she had called, and her first thought was *What did you do with the tape, you bastard?*

"The obituary will say kidney failure," Mrs. Granger

said in her hushed someone's-dead voice, "but I was in his bathroom. The medicine bottles were all out, and too many of the pills were gone. I think he committed suicide."

"Probably not," Nora said. She spoke in her calmest, surest, most nursely manner. "What's more likely is that he became confused about how many he'd taken. He may have even had another stroke. A small one."

"Do you really think so?"

"Oh yes," Nora said, and had to restrain herself from asking if Mrs. Granger had seen a new video camera around anywhere. Hooked up to Winnie's TV most likely. It would be insane to ask such a question. She almost did anyway.

That night, in bed. Their last Brooklyn night.

"You need to stop worrying," Chad said. "If someone finds that tape, they probably won't look at it. And if they do, the chance they'd connect it with you is so small as to be infinitesimal. Besides, the kid's probably forgotten it by now. The mother, too."

"The mother was there when a crazy lady assaulted

her son and then ran away," Nora said. "She'll never forget it."

"All right," he said in an equable tone that made her want to hike her knee straight into his balls.

"Maybe I ought to go over and help Mrs. Granger neaten the place up."

He looked at her as if she were mad, then rolled away from her.

"Don't do that," she said. "C'mon, Chad."

"No," he said.

"What do you mean, no? Why?"

"Because I know what you think of."

She hit him. It was a pretty good thump on the back of the neck.

He turned over and raised a fist. "Don't do that, Nora."

"Go on," she said. "You know you want to."

He almost did. She saw the twitch. Then he lowered his hand and unrolled the fingers. "No more."

She said nothing but thought, *That's what you think.*

Chad finished *Living with the Animals* in July and sent the manuscript to the agent. E-mails and phone calls followed. Chad said Ringling seemed enthusiastic. If so, Nora thought he must have saved most of that enthusiasm for the phone calls. What she saw in the e-mails was cautious optimism at best.

In August, at Ringling's request, Chad did some rewriting. He was quiet about this part of the work, a sign that it wasn't going well. But he stuck to it. Nora hardly noticed. She was absorbed in her garden.

In September, Chad insisted on going to New York and pacing Ringling's office while the man made phone calls to the seven publishers to whom the manuscript had gone. Nora thought about visiting a bar in Montpelier and picking someone up—they could go to a Motel 6—but didn't. She worked in her garden instead.

It was just as well. Chad flew back that evening instead of spending the night as he had planned. He was drunk and professed to be happy. They had a handshake deal. He named a publisher she had never heard of.

"How much?"

"That doesn't really matter, babe." Doesn't came out *dushn't,* and he only called her babe when he was drunk. "They really love the book, and that's what matters." She realized that when Chad was drunk, he sounded quite a bit like Winnie in the first months after his stroke.

"How much?"

"Forty thousand dollars." *Dollarsh.*

She laughed. "I probably made that much before I got from the bench to the playground. I figured it out the first time we watched—"

She didn't see the blow coming and didn't really feel it hit. There was a big click in her head, that was all. Then she was lying on the kitchen floor, breathing through her mouth. He had broken her nose.

"You bitch!" he said, starting to cry.

Nora sat up. The kitchen seemed to make a large drunken circle around her before steadying. Blood pattered down on the linoleum. She was amazed, in pain, exhilarated, full of shame and hilarity.

"That's right, blame me." Her voice was foggy, hooting. "Blame me and then cry your little eyes out."

He cocked his head as if he hadn't heard her—or couldn't believe what he'd heard—then made a fist and drew it back.

She raised her face, her now-crooked nose leading the way. There was a beard of blood on her chin. "Go on," she said. "It's the only thing you're halfway good at."

"How many men have you slept with since that day? Tell me!"

"Slept with none. Fucked a dozen." A lie, actually. There had only been the cop and an electrician who'd come one day while Chad was in town. "Lay on, Macduff."

Instead of laying on, Macduff opened his fist and let his hand drop to his side. "The book would have been all right if not for you. I'm going to leave you and write another one. A better one."

"Pigs will whistle."

"You wait," he said, as tearfully childish as a little boy who has just lost in a playground scuffle. "You just wait and see."

"You're drunk. Go to bed."

"You poison bitch."

Having delivered himself of this, he shuffled off to bed, walking with his head down. He even *walked* like Winnie after his stroke.

Nora thought about going to Urgent Care for her nose, but was too tired to think of a story that would have just the right touch of veracity. In her heart—her *nursely* heart—she knew there was no such story. They would see through her no matter how good her story was. ER personnel always did.

She stuffed cotton up her nose and took two Tylenol with codeine. Then she went outside and weeded her garden until it was too dark to see.

He left her and went back to New York. Sometimes he e-mailed her, and sometimes she e-mailed him back. He didn't ask for his half of the remaining money, which was good. She wouldn't have given it to him. She had worked for that money and was still working for it, feeding it into the bank little by little, paying off the house. He said in his e-mails that he was subbing again, writing on the weekends. She believed him about the subbing but not about the writing. His e-mails had a strengthless, washed-out feeling that suggested there might not be much left when it came to writing. She'd always thought he was pretty much of a one-book man, anyway.

She took care of the divorce herself. She found everything she needed on the Internet. There were papers she needed him to sign, and he signed them. They came back with no note attached.

The following summer—a good one; she was working full-time at the local hospital and her garden was an absolute riot—she was browsing in a used-book store one day and came across a volume she had seen in Winnie's study: *The Basis of Morality*. It was a pretty beat-up copy, and she was able to take it home for two dollars, plus tax.

It took her the rest of the summer and most of the fall to read it cover to cover. In the end she was disappointed. There was little or nothing in it she did not already know.